He disentang[...] [...]s
feverish hands [...] wore
no underthings a[...] quandary.
Pushing up my dr[...] t face high on
my bare thighs, hol[...] with his hands on
my naked posteriors . . [...]

# A Lady of Quality

Anonymous

**HEADLINE**

# A Lady of Quality

# CHAPTER ONE

Paris! And in the month of May! What place on earth is comparable in loveliness? As I stepped out of the Gare St. Lazare onto the bustling, café-lined streets, my mind was still intoxicated with the beauties of Normandy, which the boat-train had whisked me through: its carefully cultivated terraces, its orchards gay with the pink of cherry blossoms whose sweet perfume I had thirstily drunk in through the open window of my compartment.

I obtained temporary lodgings at a quaint, sedate boardinghouse on the Rue d'Anjou, not far from the station. That evening, refreshed after my journey, I took my first walk through Paris streets. Down the Boulevard Haussmann I went and down the Rue Vignon, till suddenly I found myself alongside the beautiful Church of the Madeleine, its stately edifice so familiar to me from the many photographs I had seen in school books. I stopped and asked myself whether I was not dreaming. A spiked bar across an angle in the building with a sign warning the public against urinating in that corner (it is still there) assured me that I was no longer in the land of hypocrites. To my left stretched the grand Boulevard de la Madeleine, and just ahead, drowned in a sea of gaslights and glistening asphalt, I recognized the magnificent Place de la Concorde.

"You are in Paris at last, Louise," I told myself, "and you have renounced the country of your birth to make this one your own. From this moment forward you are French,

Louise." Louise . . . satisfactory as my name had always been to me, I felt a deep distaste for everything which linked me to Plattsburg and the past. I must adopt another. I glanced about. A street sign caught my eye. *Boulevard de la Madeleine.* Madeleine! From henceforth that would be my name.

To become better acquainted with it, I continued up the street of my namesake to the Boul' des Italiens, past the Opera, and then to the Rue du Faubourg Montmartre. Here I seated myself before one of the innumerable street cafés, sipped a glass of claret, and watched the fascinating and interminable throng of pleasure-seekers go by. Never had I seen so cosmopolitan a parade; Syrians and Turks in red fezes, now and then an Indian rajah in full turban and burmouse, Moroccan and Algerian dark-skins, handsome French officers, easily recognizable English and American tourists . . . and women. These above all! Pert, blithesome little misses, prettily dressed, rouged and lipsticked, weave their way through the crowd, plucking an arm. here and there to offer their luscious selves while the gendarmes looked on indifferently. *Ca c'est Paris.* All this, so familiar to my readers, was then new and refreshing to me. I saw at once that I would have competition in my chosen profession; but to offset this, I gathered quickly that there would be little stigma and no criminality attached to it, and this meant much.

So impatient have I been to bring my account to my beloved Paris that I have failed to mention my trip across from New York. It was by no means uneventful, as indeed, how can any fairly attractive and not too icy a lady travel alone without some interesting adventure?

On the very second day out I was presented to the captain—a handsome old rake of about fifty, retired from the British Navy and occupying his present sinecure in a social rather than a nautical capacity. His main duty seemed to be to make himself pleasant to the wives of rich travelers and thus make them partial to his company's liners. He accosted one on deck as I stood alone at the rail, watching the wake of the ship, a vanishing trail over which I would never travel again. Seeing he was the captian, I could not very well ignore him. With pointed directness he complimented me on my beauty, then asked if I was married.—No. Going to meet a fiancé? —No. Traveling with parents?—No. Friends? —No. Alone then? Ah! It was not the custom for conventional young ladies to cross the ocean alone, he reminded me. Conventions did not faze me, I told him. It was not long before the gay old dog was inviting me to share his suite for the rest of the voyage. I refused him coldly.

"But you must have some company," he insisted, "else your trip will be blooming tiresome—and I'm here to see that it is not. Would you prefer that I introduced you to some younger men than I?" I did not dare accept his offer—as I could not without hurting his feelings. He misunderstood me. "Ah, I see. You don't care for male company. Oh well, I have just the thing: a very charming and interesting woman whom you ought to get along with very well."

That same afternoon he presented me to

Madame Mona Lugini, a mysteriously beautiful Italian woman of about thirty, an opera singer by avocation, returning from an engagement in the United States to meet her husband at Cherbourg.

"Call me Mona," she insisted as soon as we were alone.

"It must be nice to be going home with a husband waiting for you," I said inanely, just to make conversation.

"Oh, men!" She snapped her fingers contemptuously. "I have to keep one just for appearances. But they do not understand us . . . say, as you and I could understand each other, *Carissima* Louise." She took my arm in a most unjustifiedly affectionate manner. "Take this hairy old sea ape who just introduced us," she went on. "From the moment the ship left New York, he has been making love to me, asking me to sleep with him. But men do not love women as women can love each other. They are just arrogant fools, out to add another conquest to their experiences. Don't mistake me. I don't mind men when there is something to be had for it, as when I favor my managers, or a critic now and then. But to go through all that mess, and pretend to enjoy it—ugh!" Her fine breasts quivered under her black satin bodice with the violence of her disgust, her breath causing her luscious bosom to fill out like sails before a wind. I had considerable difficulty getting away, so assiduous was she in her attentions.

Late that same evening, after I had retired and lay abed reading in my stateroom, the door quietly opened, and there stood Mona in a most intoxicating negligee.

12

"Can I come in for a few minutes, Louise?" she asked. I could not refuse her. She approached, shivering with a strange intense excitement, and sat on my bed. Her thin decolleté nightdress, falling away from her bosom, disclosed two full, glorious spheres of flesh as only the well-developed women of the Latin races can boast. She was so lonesome, she told me, and couldn't sleep, and just had to come in to see me. Her teeth chattered audibly as she spoke. There was a rather cool ocean breeze coming in through the open stateroom window, but nonetheless the violence of her shivering could not be explained by it alone, for she was a magnificent full-blooded woman.

"I am so cold," she confessed pitifully. "If only you would let me get into bed beside you, Louise." I am naturally too aloof a creature to relish such intimacies with a stranger, but humanity compelled me to grant her request. She joined me under the covers. Instantly her shivering ceased. She took me in her arms compellingly, fondling and kissing my breasts with a hotness that belied entirely her recent shivering.

"What on earth does this mean?" I demanded in confusion.

"It means that I love you!" she replied intensely, "with a love that transcends the mere lust of men—and yet a love that is persistently misunderstood."

I was considerably perturbed. It was all too sudden for me to reconcile myself with. But soon the pleasant, titillating warmth of her caresses overpowered my undecided objections. Soon her hands sought the hem of my nightdress . . . gently raised it, caressing my thighs as she went along. Then, slipping entirely out of her own light negligee, she pressed her burning body close to mine. Our respective breasts glided over each other with a strange, ineffably smooth and soft sensation, till they came to rest dovetailed together, one of my bubbies nested deliciously between her two hot, gorgeous globes of flesh. At the same time, her belly began writhing softly about, bestowing a glorious satiny caress with which nothing can compare. The passionate heaving of her bosom, too, kept our titties in a continual gentle, palpitating turmoil against each other.

For a time she continued thus, caressing me only with her wondrous body, her hands employed all the time at my buttocks to hold me closer to her.

To this point, our embrace might have been excused as the harmless mutual admiration of any two women similarly situated. But suddenly, she throws the covers from off the bed, extinguishes the light, returns, and forcibly separates my thighs. There was something so hypnotic in the intensity of her ardor that I could not resist her. Her desire was so palpably real, and my resistance was so tentative and weak, that it would have seemed a kind of blasphemy, a revolt against divine authority, for little me to try and stop her. Her panting breath ran before her moist kisses up my thighs like a hot windstorm before rain: the sirocco reached my cunny, now some days without visitation. A moment later her tongue entered, her arms embraced my posteriors and raised my entire love-groove to her hungry mouth, and she launched upon a divine single gamahuching that, so far as mad intensity and really abnormal passion was concerned, has never been equaled in my whole lifetime of similar experiences.

The strangest thing of all was that, unlike Nanette, she desired no reciprocal stimulation. Her sole joy was to devour my cunt with her delicious tonguings and bitings. While thus unselfishly bestowing delight upon me, she raised her own hips up and down, writhing about as if experiencing ecstasies again and again. I have never met another such exclusively active cunnilinguist. Most women will lap another only out of gratefulness for the same thing, or in exchange, or perhaps to bribe execution of the reciprocal favor. Again and again I came. She would not let up until I was screaming out with the unbearable sensitivity of my repeatedly stimulated cunt. We slept together that night.

Next morning the captain accosted us after breakfast with a knowing satyr's smile.

"I was searching for you two ladies late last night, don't you know? There was an extempore little party in my suite. The stewardess whom I sent reported *you*, Signora Lugini, as not in your room — and as for you Miss Louise, sounds so jolly strange were heard at your door that the stewardess was afraid to disturb you. Putting one blooming thing and another together, I jolly well needn't ask you two whether you slept well last night. Now what I'm aiming at is this: I'm the law on board ship, I suppose you know, and I'm not allowed to countenance such goings on. Now, tut; tut—I'm not proposing to put you two in

15

the brig, but you might at least, out of common decency, ahem—declare me in on your party. What say, ladies?"

Angrily I walked away. I would have slapped him, had I not been restrained by the silly thought that to do so might constitute mutiny or *lesé majeste* of a sort. Mona remained behind to give him a piece of her mind—though it was a piece of another nature that he sought.

When she rejoined me, it was to report that he had continued his indecent proposals in all seriousness, urging that he could give either or both of us a much better time than we could bestow upon each other. What British bluntness! After thinking it over, I decided it was all quite funny: "Let him pant," I said, but at the same time, I made Mona promise not to join me again that night, in case there should be any further eavesdropping.

Night came. Once more I lay abed reading. Again the door opened, and there stood Mona, despite the promise I had exacted from her. I was very angry with her, and told her so; but so convincingly did she picture for me the tortures she suffered when sleeping alone, the nightmares and phantasms that beset her highly-strung imagination, that once again I had to grant her admission to my bed. Immediately she takes up her subtle caressing and mad rubbing. Soon she has stripped, doused the lights, and is between my thighs, quieting my fears with a repetition of the delights of the preceding night.

I was just on the verge of my orgasm when I was frozen with horror by a sound at the door. It opened. Someone entered quickly. The

16

door shut again. By the partial light that sifted in through the transom-ventilator from the corridors, I made out the glistening uniform of the captain. Mona had her back to the door and was too absorbed in her dear task to note his entrance.

"Heave ho, my hearties!" he spoke in a voice full of insolent assurance—too easy success with other women no doubt made him this way. "I was making my evening round of inspection and just stopped in to see how my two young charges are coming along. Ripping nice, I should say, from what I can make out in the dark. A pretty picture you do make —but what say to my finishing it up for you in the grand way intended by the good Lord Almighty?"

Mona raised her mouth from its delicious occupation only long enough to snarl these words in a low tone, "Get out of here! We don't need your help, you beef-eating British bastard!"—and like a tigress that cannot be lured off its prey, her mouth seizes again upon my cunt and goes on, sucking and nibbling as if there had been no interruption.

The intruder whistled softly and came closer. "All right! All right! Come now, Mona—I shan't interfere. But you might be a little more hospitable . . ."

He was silent for a while. Mona continued her mad tonguing; but I now had some difficulty in catching up to where we had been, with that dim masculine form looming in the darkness.

He approached still closer. As what dim light there was came from behind him, I could make out his every move—which I marked with an unearthly fear that was quite absurd, considering that neither of us had either maidenhead or chastity to lose.

His hand went down and felt the white heaving posteriors that projected over the foot of the bed.

"How nice! How nice!" he said. "Is this Mona or Louise?" Neither of us made answer; both of us were speechless, though from differing causes. There was a moment's silence, during which I could hear, above the slight pulsating of the ship's engines, only the soft liquid lapping of Mona's tongue, the heavy breathing of the horrid intruder, and the slight rasp of his coarse hands upon the ivory smooth buttocks that met his caress. He spoke again, now very nervously: "I say . . . if no one is going to claim this, I'll take it myself."

I expected Mona to fly up and scratch his eyes out; but whether in consideration for me, or in oblivion to all but her sweet task, or perhaps from plain indifference, she said not a word, confining herself more closely to the conversation in that dear language of love which held her so spellbound to my cunt.

In dim silhouette I could see the captain whip out a huge truncheon of a member. Then, raising Mona's entire lower body with his easy strength, he forced her legs wide apart till each of her feet rested upon his shoulders. Mona groaned with rage; but like a leech would not let her mouth be torn from me. Her hands clasping my buttocks more fiercely, she dug her nails into me as if to anchor herself against all the forces in the world.

What a mad scene to transcend the imagination of the most fargone erotomaniac! Within the inverted angle of Mona's luscious thighs, white and almost phosphorescent in the semi-darkness, I caught another momentary glimpse of his glistening bar as it slipped down between those widespread thighs till it found the narrow place of origin.

I could hear his stentorous breathing; I could picture his amorous fumbling as he sought the breach and lodged lip-deep in this madly ingenious position;—I could not help but feel the fierce plunge that sent him gliding home into Mona's most intimate inners, and brought him up with a dull fleshy thud as his mount met her upturned arse, as her mount met his balls in this provocative novel upside-down connection.

"Louise! Mona!" he was gasping as he lunged in and out, his quavering accents testifying at once to the extreme delight he was experiencing and to the fact that, my face in complete shadow, he still did not know which of us he was raping! It was a situation to court madness. The worst having been accomplished, I yielded myself completely to Mona's titillations, to the whole unutterable lewdness and salacity of the scene. He was fucking me, for all he knew, and though his prick was in Mona's cunt, I was experiencing all the exquisite stimulations of that heavenly act. By substitution, by transference—oh, how can I explain it, dear reader, so involved, so diabolical, so divine was it I felt as if he were really doing it to me. More—since his very thrust forced Mona's whole mouth closer into my cunt, I shared the identical rhythm of the act.

What a delicious complexity of movements, as I joined in with the other two, my hips screwing downward to Mona's mouth as he shoved her firmly toward me! It was his thrust that I was meeting. If his monster organ had torn its way clear through her passion-tossed frame till, through her mouth it had met my cunt, I could not have been fucked more effectively. To top this lascivious thought was the realization that I was being both fucked and cunt-lapped at the same time. At one moment Mona was a mere impersonal agency to my connection with that fierce fucking man which we crushed and tore apart between us. At another moment she was my dear, tender female lover, allowing herself to be raped rather than suffer my pleasure to be interrupted.

Add to this indescribable commotion of our senses and bodies the vibrations of the ship and the incessant rocking contributed by the waves, which now, whether in sympathy or by coincidence, or perhaps because I was just becoming aware of them, seemed to increase in wildness with the strong surge of our passions.

With such sights and sounds and thoughts and feelings lashing on my lustful senses, it did not take long for that earlier fear-frozen discharge still stored within me to melt and gain release through the tingling of all my fibers and the ecstatic quivering of my limbs. Down to Mona's avid mouth my twitching womb and vagina poured a flow of love's secretions that a man could not much outdo, so increased was it by the delay and by the unusual lasciviousness of our triple effect.

But Mona, gurgling in her throat with joy for my joy, does not stop at administering a single stroke of love's exquisite dying fit, but goes right on—and soon my pleasures begin anew. As for herself, she seems to be coming continuously in a ceaseless spasm of spending. There are such women, who, at times of sexual excitement can bring themselves on at will again and again—and so it was with her.

The captain, not for one moment inactive during all this, but slow in reaching his climax because of his advanced years, now gasps, "Jove! What pleasure! Mona—Louise—whichever you are—I am coming! Push closer to me! Now! Ah! Ah! gods! Ahhh!" And with the furious short plunge that accompanied each violent exhalation, I could almost see and feel the great hot jets of sperm that were shot into Mona's cunt, inverted to receive and hold every drop of it—which yet, as I found later, overflowed bounteously her belly and buttocks and dripped great gobs of it, like tallow, on the floor at the foot of the bed.

Mona, as if nothing had happened, kept up the delicious caresses of her tireless tongue and the wild writhing of her hips.

"Stop! Stop!" the captain groaned. "Are you trying to pump my life's blood out of me? —or do you want to wrench my part off? Stop, I say, you insatiable siren, until I pull out at least!"

It chanced just then that the motion of the ship changed perceptibly and it seemed that the engines had gone dead from some cause or another. The captain withdrew his dripping rammer hurriedly, replaced Mona's thighs on the bed and dried himself.

"Sorry. Must leave you ladies. Navigation requires my attention," he muttered as he stumbled out of the dark stateroom.

When Mona had finished me a second time, she arose and turned on the light. Thick, creamy fluid was trickling down her thighs. She made a move of distaste.

"Do you have a douching syringe, Louise?" she asked. "It would be funny if I became pregnant by that beast. I guess he thinks I enjoyed that swollen piece of meat crammed into me; but if I came, Louise, it wasn't due to his efforts, but to that delicious cunt of yours." So she hadn't enjoyed his wonderful fuck after all!

Next day the captain accosted me once more while I stood alone on deck. I had intended ignoring him completely; but somehow, my dreams of the night before had been entirely of being loved in that exotic wheelbarrel fashion by a vigorous, slow-coming, fully matured man.

"I say, tell me," he asked, "was it you or Mona that I had so deliciously last night?" In fairness to my friend, I could not claim credit for it, so I refused to say. He took it as an admission, and there was no use telling him otherwise.

"By Jove, you were great," he said, "but we could do much better if we two were by ourselves, don't you know. Tonight at my suite, aye what? And I'll have some bloomin' fine champagne; two bottles of Heidsick Monopole '89." Something compelled me to play up to his impression of me.

"Supposing I did meet you—what's in it for me?" I queried provocatively. I decided that I might as well start right in to learning how to handle men if I was to make a success of my life.

"Ho! ho!" he laughed in his rough, John Bull manner. "What's in it for you? I s'y, that's quite funny. What's in it for you eh? Why, if you don't mind my telling you, there'll be a fine stiff John Thomas and a good copious injection of the sap of life, by Jove!"

"By Jove!" I angrily mimicked his detestable self-assurance, "your employers may pay you to amuse the old ladies on board in that way, but I'm attractive enough to take my pick of the youngest and handsomest men on board—if that's all I wanted."

"Oh, I see," he muttered, hurt in his vanity for all his thick skin, "you want to be paid. Well, I've never done this before, but I suppose your kind have to live too. How much do you want me to pay you?"

"I don't want you to pay me anything," I answered, confused by the strangeness of being asked my price, and utterly unprepared in the methods of bargaining, "but I don't like the idea of flattering you by being just another woman who has given you what you want. So let's not say anything more about it." And I walked away.

In my stateroom, I found a note to report at the purser's office. "You haven't turned over your passport for inspection yet, Miss —"

"Passport?" I put in fearfully, "I have no

passport. I intend becoming naturalized in France."

"But have you a permit of the French immigration bureau? Without one or the other, I'm afraid you won't be able to get by the port officials at Cherbourg. Perhaps you'd better speak to the captain."

In a frenzy I sought out the old satyr. As I entered his office, he came out of a corner where he had been squeezing a young Irish stewardess. She left hurriedly, leaving her neckerchief behind her. I told him my predicament. In his best official manner he told me that I would be deported immediately upon landing and that he would probably have the pleasure of my company on the return voyage. I burst into tears.

"Well, well," he put in, human once more, "if you were a good friend of mine, I could vouch for you personally to the immigration authorities and everything would be spiffy. Only you've just refused to be nice to me, and so I suppose you'll have to ship for another voyage till we do become acquainted."

I was sport enough to admit myself fairly beaten. My tears evaporated, and my prettiest smile adorned my features. "Dear Capsie! Tonight then, in your suite?"

"No!" he roared. "Not tonight, and not in my suite, but right here and now, by Jove!"

"By Jove, Captain, you are a dear boy!"

He locked the office door. After that we got along wonderfully. Of course there was a fine sofa in the room, but when the preliminaries and stripping had been accomplished, I shamelessly confessed that I wanted it done wheelbarrow fashion.

"So you liked it after all, last night, aye what?"

"No. It wasn't me."

That put an extra edge on his appetite.

"I'll be able to tell in a minute. My dog has a better memory than I. He can always scent the difference where I can't." And he presented to my touch an instrument that completely defied my grasp and blasted all my misconceptions of sexual vigor being exclusively youth's monopoly.

A sofa cushion was placed on the richly rugged floor. Upon this I positioned my folded arms. With scarcely an effort, my gallant grasped my thighs and placed them about his hips were I locked them firmly for the time. In a moment I became accustomed to the slight strain of the upside down position. My breasts, though not naturally pendulous, now swung back and caressed my chin. Looking backward between them, and under my belly, I could see what was being done. The strange topsy-turviness of the lewd pose served only to inflame me with impatient desires; to have the barrow hitched to the rider in that equivocal cart-before-the-horse gallop we were about to set out on.

His belaying pin lay ready, pressed up against my belly by its own tension. Loosening my thighs a little to allow himself to draw back somewhat from the breach which lay so fairly before him downside-up, he lodges the thick swollen knob between the outer lips. Then, the proper direction determined, and his hands no longer needed for steering, he grasps my thighs and slowly draws my buttocks to him, as at the same time he steadily pushes down and inward to the crimson velvet-lined cavern of love. Moist and well prepared as that part was for his reception, however, never had it entertained so bulky and exercise-strengthened a visitor—and as he drew the sheath up over his majestically disproportionate weapon, I received so violent and painful a stretching that I burst into sobbing, regretting enough my over-adventurousness. I would have been split apart, had I not been favored by the generous lubrication afforded by my excitement and by the natural elasticity and adaptability that healthy young women are blessed with in those parts.

"Don't cry, child," the captain comforted me. "You'll be all right in just a minute. No . . . it wasn't you last night. I haven't been in one so nice for as long as we both, Thomas and I, can remember." And he held still for a time, savoring and enjoying the unusual constriction of the tight but moist and hot sheath.

Then, as the wet, juicy folds adjusted themselves to the huge object that engorged them, he slowly withdrew part way to allow my blood to resume circulation at the parts from which his bulk had forced it out, and then he slid all the way home to the hilt, in the living, luscious flesh cylinder that gripped him so closely and deliciously. His succeeding motions gave him no more difficulty than what served to increase his enjoyment.

The great advantage of this unique position for intercourse, dear reader, is this: that the clitoris, ordinarily situated above the love grotto and receiving only the most glancing and momentary frictions of the lover's organ (unless he rides very high, and even this has its limitations), is in the reverse position immediately beneath the beloved male joy-giver, which, instead of sliding back and forth on the lower fornix of the cunt, rests and rides continually over the tender head of the clitty. Come what may, there can be no blundering missing stroke, and this, regardless of the shape, thickness, length or even stiffness of the masculine indispensable. So much for the advantages accruing to the tenderer participant in the dear duel. As for the man who is good enough to favor his lady-love with this delicious variation, there is this recompense. The underside of his penis being the most sensitive part of him, he can feel the spongy little nodule of the clitty stiffening and bounding up and counter-stroking the delicate groove directly beneath the acorn-shaped head of his prick. As he shoves all the way home, the divine little female finger traces an exquisite little tickling line straight down the shaft of his member to the very root, reversing and repeating the delightful titillation at every stroke, giving and receiving pleasure simultaneously.

Now you can better visualize our enjoyment, envious reader. What strain there might have been in sustaining our rather acrobatic positions merely served to increase the lubricity of the act and the violence of the contrast when the final downpouring relief came. But between the beginning and the delicious end, there was an infinity of sensations that defy description. Firmly, back and forth, the captain drew and plunged his broad satisfying instrument, like the wielder of a bow on a bass-viol, never once losing contact with those strings that sent reverberating chords and harmonies of pleasure through me.

Soon my eyes glazed over and became dim with the approaching ecstasy. I could no longer discern that red blood-gorged joy-dispenser as it plunged in and out up there between my thighs. Then suddenly, I went stone blind. The rich, hot, climactic flood of sensation went eddying and sizzling through my veins, contracting all my visceral organs and causing me to faint away momentarily with the glowing overpowering sensations that inundated my brain.

I collapsed upon the cushion; but the captain continued to sustain me, slowing up his motion to a gentle massage of my inner vagina and the mouth of my enspasmed womb until I should recover. The entrance muscle of my cunt was so rigidly clamped about his member that he could scarcely move at all. But as the last waves of agonized pleasure passed away, my organ relaxed once more from its attempt to hug its delicious intruder to death.

Now gradually letting out sail and picking up speed, the captain rides along at a spanking clip before the full blast of his own desires. But before his slow, majestic ship has entered the harbor of ecstasy, the seas of delight have again risen to flood tide within me, and we share the stormy motions of pleasure together, give and take, back and forth, his pumps working furiously, and finally inundating me even further with his hot copious effusion as I drown in bliss.

As he took a last farewell plunge into my flooded hold, his creamy sacrifice, suddenly displaced, frothed over my outer cunt and hairs, sending a warm trickle across my arse and down the small of my back to my very shoulders—a generous oblation that was not, however, unmixed with some slight offering of my own, in the form of some pink and scarlet streaks of my cunt's intimate blood.

When I was dressed and taking my leave, he again assured me that everything would be arranged with the French officials.

"Now that there's no longer any need of hypocrisy between us, shall you come here tonight?" he asked.

"Mona might be suspicious," I told him. Jealous, is what I meant.

"Well, let's make it tomorrow afternoon again—between luncheon and tea."

I agreed.

Dear reader, a cunt may be a snob when some strange cock is concerned, but when once the first introduction is affected, all social distinctions and barriers are down, the better she likes it. Forty years of the captain's service in His Majesty's Navy hadn't been for nothing. In the five days that remained to our voyage, the captain demonstrated upon me the essence of this forty years of experience. But when he had tried everything from the Argentinean to the Zulu method, geographically and alphabetically inclusive, his fingers still fondled my tiny rear entrance rather longingly. A sailor will always be a sailor, I thought, but paid no further heed.

Our last afternoon together arrived. He was quite fatherly and most solicitous of my future welfare. I confessed my purpose of becoming an exclusive *vendeuse de l'amour* in

Paris—in blunt language, of living by my cunt. He laughed and promised to give me letters of introduction to some wealthy prospects. "But," he went on, "not to seem discouraging, cunt is now *tout passe*—out of fashion—in Paris."

"What do you mean?" I asked anxiously, not believing him, but yet disturbed at the implied threat to my plans.

"They are a sophisticated people, the French. Naturally, with time and excess, a whole populace may become relatively jaded and blasé toward the conventional sexual pastimes. Then begin the practice of various refinements—or 'perversions,' as the Anglo-Saxon mind is apt to consider them. But don't be frightened. There's nothing that a bright little girl can't learn in time."

"Oh! So you haven't taught me everything?"

"I'm afraid not. But there's still time for one more lesson, the pupil willing.

"You understand French? *Votre prochaine leçon, c'est faire l'amour en cul.*"

If I hadn't understood his words, his hands, creeping from my thigh where it had been resting, around to my coveted bum-hole, was explicit enough. I blushed.

"Oh, Captain!" I exclaimed, "do you mean that this huge thing (indicating the weapon that was generally in evidence whenever I was about) can be introduced into that tiny place where I cannot even insinuate a finger? Oh no! it would kill me."

"Darling child, you little understand the wonderful possibilities of the human body—especially of a woman's body. It is only at the very entrance that it is so tight—and even that is very stretchable. Beyond that there is nothing to hurt." His knowledge of anatomy was correct. It is only the sphincter or anus muscle that seems so impenetrable. Within is the wide mucous-lined rectum or sigmoid, in size and shape very much like the vagina. He prevailed upon me to let him try it. I might more wisely have waited for a less monstrously sized lover to take this, my second maidenhead; but somehow, it seemed to me especially appropriate to have this operation, smacking as it does of male homosexuality, performed by an authoritative naval man. My literary and dramatic sense has betrayed me again and again, but all through life I have acted and chosen situations as if for a projected autobiography. And sure enough, here it is.

Gloatingly and dotingly, as usual, the captain removed each article of my clothing, pausing to admire my disarray at each stage. When he could remove no more from me, he proceeded to doff his own clothes. Then, having me kneel on a soft cushion at the side of the couch, with my body leaning over it and my buttocks projecting at right angles, he went in search of some pomade—to ease his entrance, as he explained.

Like one condemned, with his head upon the block, I awaited the executioner. I entertained but little expectation of pleasure—indeed, rather expectation of great pain; but a sort of wicked curiosity, the wish to see whether this unnatural thing could be done, kept me—as yet—from relenting. Anyhow, I told myself, I wanted to savor to the dregs every experience that life had to offer—and since I would be persuaded to do this sooner or later, why not at once?

He returned with a jar of scented vaseline. Kneeling on the cushion behind me, he gently applied the soothing lubricant to the pink, puckered little exit that he so enterprisingly meant to employ as an entrance—the needle's eye through which he hoped to pass a camel —patiently dilating the exclusive little muscle with his middle finger and working in the vaseline. At first I was miserably embarrassed by his intimate handling of that most personal part of me. (I say "personal" because, unlike my cunny, I could not think that it was meant for two.) But soon, the caressing of that zone more sensitive and erogenous than I had ever dreamt, became so pleasing that I was wriggling my hips with anxiety for him to get started, though the Lord only knows what pleasure I expected to derive from it.

At last, satisfied with these preliminaries, the captain oils his own part, from head to root, which, as I glance across my shoulder to watch the procedure, seems, unless I am really seeing it for the first time, almost twice as large as it had been before. I buried my face in the sofa cushions to see no more.

Now he brings the weapon to bear upon the tiny, crinkled crevice. Two or three times it slips down the groove of my buttocks toward that other cavity where it more rightfully belongs. He brings it into position once more. But this time it flies upward at his earliest pressure. Guiding it with his hand then, so as to restrain its merest slip, he brings just the tip of his huge arrow to the tiny aperture, and slowly, firmly presses inward. This time he succeeds in gaining the entry of half the head —as I know soon enough by the horrible, unendurable agony I suffer as that narrow passage is so cruelly distended. At the same time, the muscles of that part contract rigidly—to force out the terrible foreign object that is being crammed into its disproportionately small entrance. But the captain, expecting this, counteracts it with the pressure of his body, fully holding his own.

"You must relax, Louise," he tells me, "and not try to force it out."

"Oh no! I can't stand it! Captain, you hurt me dreadfully! Oh! How you are torturing ME!" I cry tearfully. "Please, please—stop! Oh, you are tearing me open! I'll do anything; but not this! Oh! Oh!"

"Now, now!" he comforts me, "as soon as the head gets by, the distention will not be so great. Come now, relax, and press toward me. Take it in as slowly as you like—or as quickly as you can endure it." And at the same time, to divert me from the local agony which has me writhing and beating the cushions with pain, he puts his arms about my waist, and slips a finger into the top of my cunt. The dear clitty does not fail as a universal anesthetic. As the pleasure from his light, quick massaging increases, the pain fades, and soon my motions change to a back and forth movement which, with his gentle pressure from behind, soon has his whole tool sheathed in my rectum to the very root. The vaseline it was that allowed its huge bulk to slide all the way in without bruising or further pain. I felt a most indescribably peculiar sensation of being full up . . . and a slight desire to evacuate—which, however, quickly changed to a desire to hold that great bar of flesh within me indefinitely.

Now he withdraws halfway and presses in again, his movement easy and unobstructed. The caress to my soft inside passage is anything but unpleasant; only the entrance is still somewhat sore.

Very slowly and relishingly he takes each stroke.

"Oh, how close and hot—and soft—and moist it is in there!" he says. "I confess, though, it takes me half an hour to come in a cunt but when I do this, I come almost immediately." And he stops his motion again to keep the climax from overtaking him to soon. "Tell me when you are ready, Louise," he whispers, and, with his arms drawing me closer to him, he continues the rapid digital stimulation of my cunt.

"I am coming soon, Captain!" I soon gasp, as the divine dissolution approaches. He resumes fiercely the full plunge and draw and thrust into my behind—the swelling, fleshy curves of my buttocks alone protecting me against the violence of his contacts. "Now! Now!" I cry. "Oh! Oh!" As the exquisite climax enthralls me, I feel innumerable jets of hot thick sperm shooting out from his thick vibrating member, seeming to flood all my bowels, all the secret recesses of my body. We have come off simultaneously, and I kneel there bathed in thankful bliss as well as in his generous effusion, till the exquisite turmoil subsides.

His member is still hard and stiff. He begins moving back and forth within me again.

"If I pulled it out now," he explains, "the greater size of the head over that of the shaft would hurt you again—like drawing an arrow from a wound. It would be better to wait till I get soft. It won't take me long to come a second time."

And he continues, more easily than ever now, what with the additional lubrication of his part by his own generous ejaculation. True to his word, in scarcely more than twenty of his strokes, pleasant to me, divine to him, I feel another, though less prolific, injection of his warm, tingling love juices—and almost immediately his terrible engine begins shrinking, permitting the relaxation of my own dilated part until, with no difficulty at all, he draws it out of my cream-gorged bottom. The deed was done—and I was now the proud possessor of two separate and distinct bodily cavities, each for the full and complete celebration of the rites of Venus. My newer cunt I even felt some predilection for, insofar as its use entailed no fear of pregnancy and no contraceptive precaution. As for after effects, there were none. After bathing, I found my rear just as prettily puckered and chastely closed as ever. No sacrifice to love is long regretted.

# CHAPTER TWO

Back in Paris now.

After a week or so, during which I get my bearings and exercise my French, I call upon one of the references the captain has given me. He is a handsome French-Jewish banker of about thirty-five, closely related to the famous Rothschilds. He carefully reads the ambiguously worded note that I bring him with his friends recommendations. Adjusting his monocle and caressing the ends of his carefully cultivated moustache, he looks me over with friendly deliberateness.

"A little American girl in need of a friend, I see." He speaks English carefully, though not faultlessly, with a decided French accent that I become fond of at once. "And not so bad. You have come at the right time. My last mistress has recently joined the Folies Bergeres, thanks to my efforts, and now she is so much in demand that I cannot get near her even. And for a man of business responsibilities like myself, it is not advisable to stand waiting around stage doors. I must have my little woman always ready for me, whenever I can get what you call—the freedom. Do you mind if I ask you to remove your wrap and walk around the office for me to see—ah, pardon—the figure?"

Very much embarrassed, for such frank dealings were still beyond my experience, I complied. Very calmly and appraisingly he looked me up and down.

*"Ravissante! Superbe!"* he exclaimed in approval. "Now, mademoiselle, do you mind—

ah, forgive me, to bend over so, as if to tie your shoe string?"

I began to assume the required posture, until its purpose occurred to me. I stopped—and burst into tears. (By this time the reader will conclude that tears are my favorite device. I am beginning to think so myself.)

He sprang up and took me by the shoulders. "Mademoiselle! Ah, forgive me! How have I hurt you? Please! I cannot stand to hear a woman cry. I have the soft heart. What is it?"

And I spoke the lines, now so familiar as to weary the reader, but yet constituting one of the most valuable tricks in the whole of a woman's repertory.

"I am a good girl! (sobs) Of course I am willing to be nice to a kind man who will be good to me and protect me. But you parade me back and forth and examine me as if—as if I were a horse that you were going to purchase outright. Will you help me on with my coat sir? I must be going . . ."

"What! Let you go out alone and unprotected in this wicked city—you who have no friends? Ah no, Mademoiselle! All my life I would feel responsible for your fate. I am sorry if I have offended you. Stay, I implore you."

He was a very fine gentleman, for all that his English seemed to derive from effete Victorian novels. I remained. We dined together. I drank just enough wine to make it seem logical for even the best little girl to forget herself. He took me to a quiet hotel. I pretended to be horrified at the idea of being alone with a gentleman. As a matter of fact, I was raring to go—only—business first. Piece by piece, I let him undress me. I was discovering that pretended modesty is the one piquancy that the Frenchman doesn't get much of. It worked like a charm. When I snatched up my chemise, which he had just removed from me, and wrapped it across my bosom, he implored me on bended knees to uncover my charms for his admiration—and when finally I did, he pounced upon them as if these were the first bubbies he had ever set eyes upon, molding and squeezing them passionately with his hands, deftly sucking and nibbling the tiny ruby sentinels that stood stiff guard upon each of my snowy mountains.

Then, to my surprise, as he gently forces me upon my back, he spreads wide my legs and places a full gallant kiss upon my cunny, at the very juncture of its lips.

"Oh, don't do that!" I cried.

"Every polite Frenchman will do as much for any attractive lady," he told me. "And what harm can there be in thus paying one's respects to the delicious little place that is soon to bestow so much pleasure?"

Drawing forth his weapon, which was of normal size and tolerable thickness but lacking in the red cap or foreskin which it is the custom of his race to remove for hygienic purposes (my first kosher cock), he places the unencumbered ruby head between the crimson lips of my cunt, still moist from his kiss.

In the preceding days I had prepared for just such an occasion by again bathing that part, so distended by the captain's maunderings, with solutions of alum and other restorative astringents—until by now all its folds were so contracted and tightly drawn together that there was no visible or even tangible opening. Consequently, his entrance met with every impediment that real virginity could afford. With the vanity that is natural to every man, my gallant was only too willing to credit me—and more especially himself—with my maidenhead. By the naive awkwardness of my movements, I did everything to further this illusion and hinder his too-easy progress—so successfully that one of the minor folds of my vagina, bruised by the forcible entry of his part, yielded up that slight sacrifice of blood that no man is so unsadistic as not to enjoy the proofs of, and not to love his victim all the more because of it.

With our parts completely coupled at last, however, I had neither purpose nor inclination to overdo my role of innocent.

"My beloved ravisher!" I exclaimed, adopting his own dated English as the most convincing idiom, "how large and strong you are! Oh what fires you kindle in my blood! Oh! Oh! Stop—it feel's so good! No! Come into me further! Further!" And I wrapped my legs tightly about his back to give and take the best of the situation. Lust is the motive force of which love is but a single refinement. It was not difficult to pretend the one when I felt the other so strongly. It was almost inevitable that the two things, if two they be, should be so confused that I felt sincerely the sentiments that began as mere words and gestures of pretense. And so, were I to give a verbatim report of the wild and foolish terms of endearment that we showered upon each other, it would seem empty and improbable, if not preposterous. Only the actual delirious joys of prick in cunt carry and receive the conviction we both felt. Only the divine joy-filled motions of the act itself can make of all of life one great indubitable truth.

Out and in his throbbing member plunged in the tight quivering encasement of hot flesh that so hugged him in, held him back, and always invited his return. Back and forth I writhed to add every conceivable counter-caress to his blood-gorged sensitive joy-distributor, as well as to give my avid clitty the maximum of furious action. So effectively did I do the latter that I came to my supreme ecstasy some moments before him. Then, as my own pleasure subsided and I felt him stiffening all over and employing the short panting jabs that heralded his climax, I slipped a hand down between us, arched up to meet his descending body, and just as he withdrew for what I can always judge infallibly as the final masterstroke, I seized his bursting weapon, wet with my own effusions, and drawing back my body, snatched it out from its warm nest, just as he ejaculated his hot torrent of creamy essence upon my white heaving abdomen, up to my very breasts.

Two thoughts had at the last moment led me to this expedient. First, that it would not be advisable to be entirely abandoned at the first engagement. A little girlish fear would go well with his present impression. Secondly, I had taken no precautions against impregnation, and there was no use in taking needless chances when things could be finished satisfactorily enough this way.

Monsieur R., after he recovered from the

soft spasms of his pleasure, took it all in good manner. I, on the other hand, pretended to be suffering deep remorse.

"It was the wine, monsieur, that betrayed me this way, I swear it. And now that you have had your will of me, I suppose you are through."

"*Ma cherie!* I should say not! If only you are willing, I shall take care of you. I shall be your good papa. You will want for nothing."

In a few days I was set up in a luxurious apartment on the Avenue Wagram. Henri, though unmarried, warned me in advance that his business and his family claimed so much of his attention that he would be unable to spend as much of his time with me as he might like. On the very evening of our proposed "housewarming" he was two hours late. When at last he bustled in, he smacked his lips at the array of delicacies and cold viands that I had had sent up from a nearby café. He embraced me tenderly. Then, immediately proceeding to take possession of my personal charms, he asks (in French, for on my account we had agreed that it would be best to use only that language):

"What of our appetizer, dear Madeleine-Louise?" And seating himself in a soft armchair, he drew me down upon a hassock at his feet.

"Appetizer? Dear Henri, I'm afraid that I don't understand. *Nous avons des hors d'oeuvres...*"

"No. I don't mean anything like that."

"But I am anxious to please my kind protector."

"And I am always forgetting what an innocent little booby you are still. Well, if you love me, Madeleine, you will allow me the pleasure of teaching you." He opened his trousers and brought out his stiffening weapon of amorous warfare. As I sat at his feet, it threatened me to my face.

"Now, do you hate and fear this part of me?" he asks smilingly.

"No, m'sieur. I love it and—love it. It has been so good to me these last few days, giving me pleasures I have never tasted before."

"Fine. Then you needn't shrink from it. Take it in your hand, fondle it, show your appreciation." I complied, rubbing and stroking it timidly with my palm, closing both my hands about its shaft till only the scarlet head protruded, and squeezing it gently till a tiny drop of precoital fluid appeared at its mouth. The whole of it felt so strange, warm, smooth and pulsating to my grasp that I was in reality somewhat awed by my proximity to this male charmer, although it had already plumbed to my vitals some six times at least since we had met. It did not take long, however, for me to feel quite at home in handling it—although, indeed, my manipulations were considerably restrained by a fear that the highly charged capricious engine might choose to go off at any moment on my bosom, and ruin the fine gown I was wearing.

"Now, would you be very frightened if I asked you to kiss it?" A little hesitantly I complied, placing a quick kiss upon its beaming countenance. Its whole shaft tautened with a suddenness that nearly wrenched it from my hand.

"Now once more, darling Madeleine—only more like you kiss me."

I close my lips moistly about the end and gave it a long kiss, during which my tongue played it lightly back and forth across it.

"Ah! That is it, my divine woman. Look, I shut my eyes and leave it all to you. Imagine you were in my place. Do everything with your mouth and hands that you think you would like. And afterward I have a fine surprise for you." He lay back luxuriously in the chair. I felt that a great deal depended upon my ability to learn quickly.

Opening his trousers further, to bare every part of his precious instrument, I reached in and brought out even his soft tender love reservoirs, which I balanced strokingly upon my palm. Starting with the tip-top and dilating with the tiny tip of my tongue the little canal from which all blessings flow, I next placed a series of the moistest conceivable kisses all the way down the shaft to its very root. Then, returning to the place whence I had started, I ran my tongue up its whole length to the very head. This procedure of kissing and tonguing I repeated again and again, sometimes varying it by running my wet tongue up along the sides or the top of the shaft instead of underneath, sometimes encircling my tongue about its sensitive bulk in a subtle spiral that is difficult to describe but which must have been inutterably exquisite to the owner of the part so caressed.

How did I learn all this? I can credit it only to the instinct that exists in most women for anything lubricious. Soon all my self-consciousness vanished and I took an artist's pride in devising the utmost possible variations of caresses and titillations with my lips and tongue. When, from his flushed face, disturbed breathing and troubled writhing I judged—and judged correctly—my Henri to be sufficiently charged, I took to licking exclusively the soft sensitive groove immediately under the acorn-shaped head while I held the shaft tightly in my fist, much as a child handles a delicious lollipop, looking up to my lover's face for his approval. Finally . . .

"Take it in your mouth—all of it, *ma chere* Madeleine!" he gasped, yielding in his approaching extremity to the irresistible male impulse to sheath his cock in no-matter-what. With an effort, I opened my mouth wide enough to take in his bulky cylinder. He grasped my head with both his hands behind my ears and drew me closer, closer to him, until his member, touching the rearmost part of my mouth, threatened to force its way down my very throat. I pulled away a little and took hold of his reckless member with my fist, grasping it tightly just beneath the point on the thick shaft that I considered would constitute a good mouthful, or as much as I could chew. Alternately, I now sucked upon the fleshy morsel or stroked and rolled my soft tongue about its hot, throbbing head. The effect of this treatment, unbelievable as it may seem, was to swell that mouthful so prodigiously that there was no longer any room in my mouth for its further manipulation by my otherwise agile tongue. Now I was confined to sucking it and massaging the length of the staff with my hand.

As it swelled, preliminary to its final outburst, Henri shoved it forcibly back in my mouth once more, as if to drive it through my head. I tried in vain to clear my throat, so engorged was I with this tower of delicious living flesh.

Suddenly, with a few furious back-and-forth movements of his hips and a low triumphant cry of joy, Henri came, his organ stiffening into steel, while a hot stream of his thick love-balsam spurted in soothing torrents down my throat, filling my mouth, already swimming in saliva, to its very maximum, so that much of the creamy proofs of his enjoyment began dripping from the corners of my lips. There was only one thing to be done about it —and I hope that you will not consider me too depraved, kind reader. The thick white love-fluid, that quintessence of manhood, was smooth and pleasant upon my tongue. Its taste, if any, was ever so slightly minty and aromatic. Already much of it had gone down my throat. There was no point in being ridiculous. I swallowed the rest.

For a moment longer I continued sucking and tonguing gently, to make sure that his pleasure was all over. Another fitful little spurt of cream was my reward. It was delightful, wholly apart from the erotic element, this sucking of warm, polished, living flesh, this fruition of sweet human milk that came to my share. I felt as happy and contented as a child at its mother's breast and I could have gone on like this forever, giving great pleasure in return for a simpler one, had he not withdrawn himself, and taking me in his arms, covered my neck—and yes, my mouth— with blindly ecstatic kisses. Then, in grateful-

ness for the incomparable pleasure I had
bestowed upon him, he changes places with
me, and throwing back the tangle of my skirts
and chemise, his hot mouth still panting with
his own joy, seeks out my cunny, which, in a
not inconsiderable state of excitement from
my handling an instrument that more rightfully belonged to it, comes forward eagerly to
meet his kiss. But he intends more than this.
His strong tongue separates the adhesion of
the glowing mossy folds and finds the clitty—
and he administers to me, to the great delight
of all my senses, a divine gamahuching, so
far superior in emotional and sensual strength
to any I had yet experienced from women—
so much greater and more forceful is the passion
and worship of the opposite sex—that I was
left completely prostrated by the climactic joy,
my breast rising and falling, my limbs twitching violently, my lips emitting low involuntary
moans of pleasure, as I gasped inarticulate
words of profound endearment.

# CHAPTER THREE

Time passed. Henri was wonderfully good to me, showering me with jewels and clothes with a generosity that belied the avarice generally attributed to his race. Although not socially inclined, his influential connections frequently required his attendance at various salons, dinners and balls—and on such occasions, as is the recognized custom among the French, he would openly present me as his *petite amie* or mistress, and nothing improper was thought of it. There was none of that snobbery that characterized my debuts in New York and I was able to meet ambassadors, dukes and even princes on an even basis.

As for my excessive leisure, especially in the daytime, Henri, anxious to have me appear in the best possible light, engaged for me a tutor who, besides perfecting me in my French, gave me intensive daily lessons in German, Italian and Russian. I discovered in myself a natural propensity for learning languages—and always I was spurred on by my deep desire to travel to further lands, as well as to be able to converse with the many fascinating literary and political figures from all over Europe that I was meeting continually.

For all his kindness however, it did not take many months before I began to tire of Henri, unfortunately, before he could tire of me. The monotony of having always the expected thing done to me in lovemaking even though, besides the variants of copulation, we practiced the *mimi* he had taught me, and gamahuching, and even *l'amour in cul*—became dreadfully enervating. Women cannot generally admit to it, but if their desires are strong, they need variety in partners even more than men. Men can always get their pleasure from any old hole; but women, more subtly constructed, require a certain sympathetic harmony, a certain nervous tension, without which they begin missing thrills and become impervious to any but the most direct and prolonged frictionings.

It was inevitable then that, as other admirers, both young and old, whispered their compliments to me as we wheeled through the steps of a dance at some ambassadorial ball or another, I lent a more and more favorable ear, and became more and more susceptible to their proposals. Soon I was carrying on little afternoon liaisons with other men, any of whom would have been glad to replace Henri as my protector altogether, but who had to content themselves with a bit of fruit now and then, stolen from someone else's orchard. Many a dress shirt with diagonal silk band, glittering with military or diplomatic decorations, pressed against the tender charms of my bosom in the ensuing year.

I had many opportunities to employ in languages other than French or English the impassioned terminology of love. On my waiting list of men ready, willing and able to pay the upkeep of the expensive-tasted young lady that I had become were no less than four marquises, two barons, two dukes (one Italian and one Russian) and a prince whose nation I shall not embarrass by naming it. Quite an advancement from the naive little hayseed of Plattsburg, New York, U. S. A.! What man, be he ever so talented, ambitious and fortunate could in a whole lifetime climb the distance that a woman can traverse in a few well-engineered nights? What but cunt can aspire to the beds of kings?

Such trouble with my conscience as I was still able to suffer during these numerous little infidelities was softened in this way: many of my lovers, anxious to allay Henri's suspicions, would overwhelm him with courtesies and favors of all sorts, so that I daresay the sums he spent upon me, generous as they were, were more than amply compensated for by the valuable business concessions that, without his knowledge, a beautiful woman was bringing to him. And I was—if I must say it myself— a delicious trick at this time. About twenty-one, five feet five inches in height, a hundred and two pounds in weight, hair a bit darker than chestnut, a faultless complexion, and above all a good figure, with just the proper degree of both suavity and voluptuousness. My breasts, perfectly matured hemispheres by now, when held together by a low-cut close-fitting gown, displayed just that properly luscious hiatus or cleft between them that men find so alluring and provocative. My hips and thighs too had that quality of flowing line that so invites the hands of men to feel and verify their intoxicating curves. My ankles were slim, but with enough upward increase to assure all who looked that there was more generous plumpness above. Need I have been of royal birth or possessed of hereditary estates when such riches as these were mine?

For all my "high-society" existence, my interest in the so-called demimonde did not forsake me during this time. At every opportunity I would induce Henri or his friends to take me on varied slumming tours to the wilder and more notorious of the Paris resorts. Of course, there was the Moulin Rouge, with its swarms of the more expensive cocottes, the Bal Tabarin with its performances of the lewd "can-can" and its female wrestlers—lasciviously dressed grisettes who pretended to go through the gestures of fighting merely for the purpose of effecting various salacious poses and tableaux and inflaming the more sadistic of the onlookers, which, when done, the little ladies, edible bits enough, would circulate among the crowd and arrange for more genuine combats in private whether with male or female. And so down the whole roster of cafés, some of them specializing in male perverts, some in female perverts, most of them generalizing in everything.

One week, while Henri was away in Amsterdam on business, I had the *Duc de* ——, one of my sub rosa amours of the moment, a fascinating young rake who knew the ropes superlatively, take me through some of the more obscure places of pleasure: the House of All Nations, the Crystal Palace, and so on, where "circuses" exhibiting the practice of all the perversions under God's heaven were put on. Among the other and more usual things, a woman would allow herself to be lapped by a dog especially trained for that purpose (illuminating my mind as to the meaning of the term "lap-dog" as applied to the pets that some women are never without); another would be actually penetrated by a mule in rut; one woman, wearing a very logical rubber instrument strapped about her waist, would pierce into the inners of another girl and perform the part of man. There were more complicated exhibitions too, employing as many as eight actors at once as well as various mechanical implements, all to some lubricious purpose. I must admit that even at the outset I was more aroused than disgusted by all this—and in the aftermath, when I was at last alone with my companion, I acted like a nymphomaniac possessed by the devil, fucking and doing "sixty-nines" with mad tireless abandon, and regretting only that respectability of a sort still prevented me from handling more than one man at a time. It was on excursions like these that I gathered most of the inspiration that I was to employ later in a house of my own. I learned that there are certain postures, certain situations, that will whip up the most jaded or frozen senses—and it is entirely in the proper plotting of such lustful scenes that the casual watcher is turned into a devoted habitué, a sincere worshiper of the voluptuous Venus. In the ultimate, it is as Wilde put it: "Life is the imitation of Art." Without all the exquisite stimulations of civilization's refinements, men would still be crude bestial back-scuttling creatures with only rare periodic ruts: women would be graceless child-bearing drudges with never the remotest glimpse of sensual delights. Yet, this is the low standard that society and law would hold us down to. It is we who through the artful presentation of the glorious rhythms of the human body and the infinite possible manners in which humankind can give divine pleasures to humankind, that with Art give you greater life. Let not the eunuchs and hypocrites of church and state tell you otherwise. It is they who are the real seducers—they who will cheat you of that noble earthly birthright which partakes far more of heaven than all their inane liturgies and theologies. In the grave there are no ecstasies, no divine spasms of glowing, quivering sensate flesh; there is only oblivion and maggoty dissolution. And even if there were a Hereafter, there would alas be no houris for we poor Christians—none of the healthy sensual relaxations that the Mohammedan promises himself; there would be only more liturgies, confiteors, fast days—perhaps some psalm-singing at best. So come all ye men who are weary with the hypocrisies of life and heavy laden with the repression of natural passions, come ye all to the heaving bosom and widespread thighs of woman, and yours will be the real kingdom of heaven, the power and the glory, yours will be the real peace on earth, the happy languor and good will toward men that come only with the satisfaction of the senses. Aye, verily, it is fucking that I preach.

But I digress and become, I fear, not at all amusing. Let us turn our backs on living corpses and, making the most of life, still not fall into the error of taking ourselves too seriously. Laughingly onward, then.

Once, at one of these Temples of Eros that I describe, while the *Duc* and I watched a performance in which girls dressed as nuns were treated in a quite ungodly fashion by a number of handsomely proportioned men in cassocks whose bulging members almost convinced one that they were indeed of the Carmelite order they portrayed—one of the girls approached as we sat cooling our fevered senses in iced champagne, and brazenly unbuttoning my escort, fell to her knees before his living symbol of Priapus and proceeded to do it homage with her mouth—though not at all verbally—and with such passionate zest that one might forget her calling and imagine that she hadn't had one in years. She was really quite good—and the *Duc* could scarcely be blamed for allowing his interest to be at once aroused. He looked at me helplessly and rather sheepishly said:

"Do you mind, dear Madeleine?"

"Of course not, dear *Duc*. Enjoy yourself. And I shall turn my head away, lest my presence disturb you." As a matter of fact I was insanely envious of him. There were numerous other persons about, but they seemed only mildly amused and ignored us for the most part—from which I surmised that this form of amusement was quite customarily served at this particular café. Out of the corner of my eye I could not help but watch the maddeningly lustful little tableau. The pretty cherry-lipped young lady between his knees was a veritable witch at describing around his member strange cabalistic circles and spirals with her tongue that soon set the caldrons aboiling. And she was a vampire and succubus to boot when it came to the final stage of the *aparashtika* (as the Hindus designate this delicious rite; viz, sucking the juice from the fruit) for she did this so effectively that, after he had tipped her handsomely and we returned home, the *Duc* was so exhausted that he could not raise even a little bone for my own relief. I sent him away, pretending to be ill, and by telephone routed out Baron ——, the Ambassador of ——, in the midst of the night, and had him come right up to extinguish the raging internal fires that the evening's entertainment had kindled in me.

On a few of these exciting excursions about dear Paris, I deemed it advisable to employ the artifice of disguising my sex, as I had done so successfully in New York that New Year's Eve two years ago. One night when Henri could not come with me, I dressed up in his best street clothes (he was not much taller than I) and went alone to visit a notorious cafe on the Rue Blondel that I had heard much of. Although it was a "wide-open" place, facing directly on the street and making no pretense at concealment, the "hostesses"—over sixty of them, and every one attractive, though of varying types and builds—were all stark-nude. No sooner had I entered than the whole mob of them, excepting the few that were already engaged in dancing or toying with the men, swarmed upon me, demanding that I pick one or more of them for an immediate round of drinks and loving. I waved them aside and seated myself at a table to collect my senses.

The large hall was entirely lined with mirrors and heated to an almost stifling temperature—for the comfort of the unclad ladies if not for the temperaments of the male customers. I ordered a drink and looked about me. What an array of breasts and buttocks, ranging from the slim and petite through the pleasingly plump to the extra voluptuous! What a collection of pretty cunts, some entirely shaven and showing the whitest ivory tinged with pink at their lower convergences, others richly begrown with every conceivable shade of chevelure from lightest blonde to gold, auburn, brown and deepest sable black. They paraded about singly or in pairs to display their charms. It was a painting of an old pagan Greek scene come to life. As they passed me, some would wink, one would cup a luscious breast in her hand as if to offer it to me, another would roll her center about with a slow, sinuous, voluptuous movement and then throw it forward with spasmodic jerks as if in the very throes of spending. Yet others were demure and retiring, thus catering to every variety of taste. All in all, it was most arousing to any to whom women would at all be associated with pleasure— and I am, I confess, though by no means exclusively, one of those.

Directly opposite me, on the leather-cushioned wall-bench that is so inevitable in our Paris cafés, an elderly gentleman sat, wearing a long beard and a high opera hat. He seemed a bit under his liquor, for he sat looking forward with a totally blank stare. At each side of him two comely, naked sirens embraced and caressed him, trying to stir up in him some memory of his lost youth. "Ah, papa! Won't you come upstairs with us? We will be so good to you—ooh, la la!" But in vain. He sat there, puffing his cigar, unaffected. May you, kind friends and readers, never get that way!

Other grotesqueries were presented to my view by some of the cruder girls, who went about picking up coins from the edge of a table by the contraction of their cunnies, or actually puffing cigarettes placed between their nether lips by internal suctions. I did not relish this. Extraordinary muscular control it was, yes, but totally wasted and misdirected in clownings that deprived these parts of their natural dignity and beauty.

One of the quieter girls, unbelievably youthful and fresh in her appearance, attracted my attention. She sat not far from me, looking on wearily and a trifle disgustedly at the noisy tomfooleries going on. Though her luscious, sensuous body was undoubtedly made for love, it was obvious that she was out of place amongst these public vulgarities.

Noting that I eyed her with interest, she came over and joined me. She was a dazzling, golden-haired blonde, nude like the others except for a flimsy bit of a silk scarf that hung around her neck and floated back and forth across her breasts and secret spot, lending her an air of intermittent modesty. Her skin was flawless, bright, and smooth as alabaster; her thighs, plump but daintily and perfectly turned, were close-meeting up to the very point where they melted into her hips and belly. Her delicious delta was shaded with dark silky hair, giving that promise of intensity and passion that her chaste blonde head seemed to deny.

She put her arms about me. I did likewise to her, running my hand—with a deftness that only a woman who knows what a woman likes can employ—down her polished side to where her soft, velvety buttocks were profaned by contact with the leather seat.

"We are both young, m'sieur," she said in an indescribably sweet voice, looking at me in an exceedingly friendly manner. "Neither of us, I fear, is very familiar with this sort of thing. You look so good and innocent that I would send you home to your mother if I dared." This to me. "But if you must have a woman, I would very much like to be the one you choose." I said not a word. "I would be so much kinder to you than those more boisterous and hardened women. Do you wish to come with me?"

I nodded my head, afraid to speak and perhaps betray myself. Exactly as in my earlier adventure with Nanette, we went upstairs together. Only this time I did not wait for her to discover my real sex. I disclosed it at once. When she had recovered from her surprise, she asked what I wanted of her.

"What is your name?" I asked.

"Fleurette," she replied. The name fell from her pretty lips like the petal of a flower—the "r" flitted over with a tiny butterfly movement of the tip of her scarlet tongue that was flashingly visible through the slightly parted lines of her perfect white teeth.

"Fleurette—I want what men come for: a woman. Is there any reason why a woman who is lonely should not be able to get company in the same way as a man?"

"Then mademoiselle wants a gigolo."

"No, Fleurette. It is you that I want. You are beautiful."

"I see, mademoiselle. Personally, I am not that kind. But we girls are here to please, one way or another. I am at your service."

I took my first purchased love into my arms and kissed her upon the mouth. Before long my tender passion communicated itself to her. She responded in kind. Soon I was stripped, retaining nothing but my chemise. As she knelt between my knees, which I held widespread, she spoke in admiration.

"What a fresh, lovable little sister you have there, mademoiselle. It is like a fine fig, bursting open with ripeness." And her mouth went to my palpitating love cleft, really with the unrestrained zest of a hungry person attacking a juicy piece of sweet fruit. She was a little awkward at first, but I helped her along with my own movements, and it did not take long for her to learn. My climax came soon. It was a soft, delicate, fleecy thrill, not intense or violent, but slow and long-lasting and ineffably pleasurable.

Fleurette was even younger than she appeared—only sixteen in fact, though almost as mature as I. But her wisdom as well as her lovely body was well beyond her years. She had just a few months before taken to prostitution, as a mere matter of course. Her sister was in the profession, and there had been nothing else open to her.

"It isn't that I don't like men, mademoiselle, for frequently they give me great pleasure; but I detest the idea of taking so many different men in my arms all in one night, without the chance of becoming acquainted with any of them. I would like to be wooed, even if only for a day. And I would like to give myself in my own manner—not according to the passing whim of the stranger who pays me."

A bright idea occurred to me.

"Fleurette," I said, "how would you like to come away from here with me? I am very rich. I have innumerable lovers—so many that you could help me take care of them. You would pose sometimes as my maid, sometimes as a companion of equal social standing. I will pay you more than you can possibly earn here, you will have all the fine clothes you want, and I promise you that while you will have plenty of male company (and when not, you will have me) there will rarely be more than one a night."

"You are making fun!" Fleurette gasped incredulously.

She came away with me. She is with me still. And hardly ever, in the nine years that have since intervened, has she been for long outside the range of my voice. Faithful and unselfish, she has been my greatest single acquisition in life, my only really deep friendship. From the beginning she gave all of herself to me, in every possible capacity. As my sweetheart, her dear delicious body has always been mine in preemption of all others. As a confidante, she has always been trustworthy. When there have been little amorous intrigues to plot, raveled situations to untangle, her advice has always helped. She has even doubled for me in bed on certain dark nights, though in more recent years there has developed some disparity in our figures that makes such deceits now impossible. And so self-effacing! Never has she controverted my word. And so much trust has she placed in me that, wishing always to be dependent upon my generosity, she has persistently refused to amass any money of her own, but has placed everything in my keeping.

In those earlier years of our association she

was able to serve me most valuably in this way: whenever I tired of a master or protector, whenever the greater shares of an amour had died away and only the lesser glow remained, I would use Fleurette as a foil. Fully as beautiful as I, though in an almost diametrically opposite manner, less forceful, less compelling, I would bring her forward into the picture, giving her the highlights as it were, and allowing myself to sink into shadow. Almost invariably my man would fall for her, and the transfer of affections effected, my own severance could be made with pain to no one. Thus it is that I have never made an enemy. All of my ex-lovers are still my best friends. Sometimes I even allow them a return engagement for the sake of auld lang syne. Always they have themselves felt guilty of our separation and have been deeply grateful for my broad tolerance—which allowed them to carry on their liaison with my maid without subjecting them to the outbursts of jealousy that they expected and deemed they deserved. Consequently, in leaving me, each has always left me well provided for financially.

It was an ideal arrangement, a perfection of the technique I had used on Charley—and one which every other woman might well employ to advantage. It is better to draw off a lover than to break off with him. There are no broken hearts, no jealousies, no *crimes passionels*. And there is not a man under the skies who is not susceptible to this drawing-off process. It requires only the maneuvering intelligence of a woman who is not so narrow as to play the dog in the manger and insist on keeping the fidelity of a man whose love she would well be rid of.

Henri, of course, was the first to go by this method of painless seduction. I shall not be so conceited as to pity him. When I had approved his infidelity with Fleurette and had myself taken up with a handsome Italian duke, he paid her court openly for some months before being entirely lured away by another. Soon the Italian went the way of the others. For another six months I shared my luxurious bed with a most persistent but extremely wealthy German diplomat. It was he who presented me with my gorgeous home facing the Bois, where I still repair whenever I feel the need of indulging myself in a quiet prolonged liaison—which is rarely.

During that winter that the German's blond bullet-head lay upon my bosom or between my thighs on awakening every morning, I had to resort to the most arrant means to get away for a breath of another's passion, for he was a most jealous and possessive lover. At last, however, I succeeded in inducing my doctor (guess how!) to certify that I required a few weeks in the Alps for my health, and as my German's duties required his uninterrupted presence in Paris, I arranged with a romantic and wealthy young Spanish don, who had been paying me court assiduously, to meet him at Saint Moritz in Switzerland in a few days. On the train, going to my rendezvous, I had a thrilling little adventure that I am especially fond of recollecting, as it somehow makes me feel as if I have paid off whatever debt I might once have owed to my native America.

I had left Fleurette behind to do her damned-
est with the all-too-faithful German and I
was traveling alone—impatient to get to my
destination for an orgy of real illegitimate
fucking. Somehow I have always felt that as
soon as I belong to a man sufficiently for
him to expect my favors as a matter of arrangement or established economic right, it is
as legitimate as being married, and consequently, to one who was developing a passion
to measure with all her bodily openings as
many pricks as could possibly be crammed
into a lifetime, such a state would soon become quite tiresome. I have learned too that
no man's prick is ever again quite as thick
and upstanding as it is on its first unbelievably exquisite entrance into a particular
woman.

The train was speeding through the French
Savoy. It was night, but as yet too early to
retire. Leaving my private compartment on
the "wagonlits," I went out into the corridor
—perhaps to seek an acquaintance. But
whether the car was empty, or whether the
occupants had already turned in, there was
no one around, and there was nothing to do
but stand at the rail and watch the snow-
blanketed night landscape dance by.

Wearying of this, I went for a walk to
stretch my legs, passing back through a number of cars until I found myself in the rearmost unit, an unheated, rough, third-class carriage. This too was empty save for two or
three immigrants sprawled snoring asleep and
a lone young man who sat gloomily looking
out of the window and shivering in his thin
shabby overcoat. I don't know what it was

that drew me to him—perhaps it was my own loneliness; but I sat down opposite him and ventured to address him—in French.

*"Je ne comprend pas bien Francais,"* he replied apologetically. *"Je suis Americain."*

American! I immediately disclosed my like origin. He brightened and at once became very friendly. He was a poor student who had worked his way across to Europe late the preceeding summer, thirsting for Old World culture. Now, nearly penniless, he was on his way to Geneva in the hope of getting work as a waiter at the University so that he might attend some of its classes. He was handsome and genteel in appearance but seemed badly fed and shivered violently whenever a draft flew through the car.

"Do you sleep the whole night on these cold hard wooden benches?" I asked him. He nodded his head ruefully. I thought quickly, ballotting my desires. I was not the one to hesitate over going forth to welcome adventure with open arms.

"Young man," I said, "I don't know your name, but you are a fellow-being in distress. While you freeze to death here, there is a comfortably heated carriage up front that is more than half-empty. You must come forward with me."

"But my ticket, my clothes," he expostulated.

"I will stand responsible for that."

He accompanied me forward. I led him directly to my private compartment. When he saw my nightclothes laid out on the berth and the other personal articles of a woman's toilette strewn about, he hesitated to enter.

"Oh no. I cannot remain here and compromise you, madame," he said.

"But I wish to converse further with you—and certainly you wouldn't have me catch my death of cold in that drafty corridor? You must remain here and thaw out awhile." I removed my wrap—letting him glimpse somewhat of my upper charms as I arranged the bosom of my dress. (I might interpose that such seemingly accidental views, the drooping of a careless décolleté, an exposed area of lucent bare thigh while adjusting a garter, can be far more effective in the engineering of an amorous experiment than the very act of undressing itself. For over an hour we conversed, most interestingly and impersonally. At last he arose to leave, shivering at the mere thought of the freezing car he was returning to. I took his arm.

"You are a clean, honorable fellow, Mark," I said, "and I judged you to be so from the first moment you spoke. I can't bear to think of you out in that cold boxcar all night. If you will promise to be good, and not presume too much on my invitation, you can sleep right in here."

"But . . . but you have only one berth . . ."

"True, and I don't expect you to sleep on the floor or in the baggage rack."

He flushed, looked hungrily at my intoxicating silk-clad form and at the glowing hemispheres of my warm bosom which peeped over the edge of my bodice like a sunrise viewed by a man so drunk as to see double. Then he looked out the window at the cold snow-wrapped landscape. He stayed.

While he went to the lavatory to wash up, I undressed and put on my very thinnest silk-crepe *chemise de nuit*. When he returned, looking clean and fresh and handsomer than ever, I was already snuggled expectantly under the covers. Since he was dreadfully self-conscious about himself undressing, I instructed him to do so in the dark. He put out the light. A moment later he slipped carefully between the sheets, keeping to the extreme edge of the berth so as not to touch me. But even at that, we were so close to each other as to be within the aura of each other's bodily heat —and I knew that as my bosom rose and fell my breasts just barely touched him. I smiled to myself. "American!" I thought, "who thinks it is taking unfair advantage of a lady to share with her life's supremest joy."

An interminable period elapsed. Far from sleeping, my companion was vibrant with uncontrollable nervousness—at this no doubt unaccustomed proximity to a woman. But still he kept his promise. Finally, as if by accident, I let my hand fall upon his shoulder. He shivered violently with the excitement set off by my contact. I confess that I myself felt almost as tense as he.

"You are cold," I whispered. "Would you like to lie closer to me?"

"How dare I?" he almost groaned. But I put my arms about him and drew him close to my hot body, nestling his head against my soft perfumed bosom, and bringing my abdomen gently up to his. He was wearing a suit of light underwear that left his arms and thighs entirely bare. Through its thin cotton texture I could feel the bulk, the hardness and the heat of his member, which pressed against my thigh.

"Now you can go to sleep, dear boy." I said.

"Sleep!" he exclaimed, and crushing me suddenly closer to him, he implanted a series of burning kisses on my neck and bosom. I pushed him away, pretending to be offended.

"Is this the way you keep your promise?" I chided. "If you can't lie here, nice and friendly, without getting insolent, we will simply have to part. Come now, and be good."

I cuddled close to him once more, forgivingly, but with some primness. "Good night, Mark," I said. "Sleep well and don't think of nasty things."

All of a half-hour passed. I knew that he was yet awake, though, for fear of disturbing me, he lay very still. As for myself, I pretended to gradually fall asleep, regulating my breathing and the gentle rise and fall of my bosom. Would he be as "honorable" while I was asleep? If so, I would be dreadfully disappointed. The man who in a situation like this could resist temptation would have to be no man at all. To be stronger in honor, he would have to be weaker in healthy desires.

The time passed, silent except for the slight clatter of the train over the rails and our respective deep breathing. Through my mind kept passing all the different pictures that I guessed must be troubling the thoughts of the young man beside me. At length, I felt him stir.

"Madame . . ." he whispered. It was only to test my wakefulness. I made no response. Gently his hand came forward and felt tremblingly for my breast—which, left substantially bare by the loose droop of my nightgown, soon·rewarded his search. His heart was beating so strongly that I could actually hear its loud thumping—and my own breathing was so disturbed by the tenseness of the situation that I had the greatest difficulty carrying on my pretense.

For a while his fingers fearfully traced the outlines of my provoking bosom, cupping each tender globe gently with his palm and lightly stroking their little cherry tips ·till the usual firm erectness ensued. Then, wandering lower, his hands felt of my smooth substantial thighs through the filmy gauze of my nightdress, stroking gently around them to my posteriors, returning to feel my polished belly and the soft silky clump that marked its base and hid the hot goal of love. In all of his caresses there was a strange tense furtiveness that aroused every lascivious element in my make-up and whipped my senses to a frenzy of expectancy and anxiety.

For a time he contented himself with these contraband explorations and stolen touches; but reassured by my continued quiescence, he became more emboldened. His hands took hold of the hem of my gown and began pulling it up slowly from my knees as far as it would raise in front—which was only midway up my thighs. To the fine expanse thus uncovered, his hands went; but as if scalded by the heat of my flesh, he withdrew them—only to return after a moment's fumbling and lay upon me the even hotter throbbing bar of flesh that was his penis. Here he kept it, pressed between the blood-warmed ivory of my thighs, while with his hands he resumed the secretive fondling of my ineffably soft bubbies, which veritably melted beneath his hot touch. But his passion increased rather than decreased by this expedient, and panting softly with leashed desires, he resumed once more the raising of my light negligee, now, however, finding it necessary to pull it up from under me.

I tried to aid him by imperceptibly stiffening my body and raising my buttocks from the bed a trifle, but the pressure of one of my hips pinned down the now detestable covering. As he continued to tug gently, still not recognizing the impossibility of what he sought to accomplish, I stirred, sighed deeply, and wriggled my buttocks about somewhat, as if in a semiwaking state, till I had slipped down and out of the imprisoning strain of the chemise. Frightened, he withdrew and lay quietly for a long time, his heart pounding away as if to burst; but when my regular breathing reassured him once more, he returned to his delicious burglary, and this time, his task lightened, he soon had all of my dress well up on my belly.

I was lying on my side, facing him, and now, with the field at last clear before him, he brought his eager weapon to me, slipped it quietly up the groove of my thighs and forced it gently into the silky tangle of my mount. It slid in between easily enough, but, relax as much as I would, the contiguity of my legs kept the lips of the vital spot pressed close together, and his engine rested only on the outside of these essential soft parts.

Almost sobbing with impatience now, and yet forced to calculate and restrain every move to keep from waking me as he thought, he withdrew and proceeded with gentle force to slip his knee between my thighs. This time, hozannah! When he approaches his bursting member to me once more, the cleft is open and accessible. Carefully he places it to the breach, quartering my cunt open with his fingers till he gains partial entrance, and then, releasing the hot soft lips of the vulva which close hungrily about his shaft, he slips his hands to my posteriors, and drawing himself closer, pushes the darling bolt all the way home, nailing us belly to belly.

For a while he restrains his impatience to allow my sleeping body to accustom itself to this impenetration of his hardened flesh, then slowly he begins a rhythmic back-and-forth movement. It was lustfully maddening beyond the power of words to express. With every stroke, ungovernable impulses arose within me to give as well as to take, to heave, to writhe, to dance the immortal dance of love. Movement became as necessary to me as to him. I could no longer carry on my pretense of unconsciousness.

I stirred—awakened.

"Oh! What is this?" I exclaimed. "What are you doing to me? Go away, you—you base ravisher!" But I took care that my push did not dislodge him.

"Dear lady—I would have to be inhuman to be able to resist you. Please! Let me have you willingly—for if I hang for it, I must have you!" And goaded on by his urgent desires, he resumed his strong back-and-forth motion within my humid grotto.

"But what of my husband?" I lied, permitting myself a frantic little motion of the hips that was not at all meant to discourage him.

"Oh, oh! What will I do?" I cried—doing it. "And anyway, you are hurting my leg. You might at least lie over me in a decent fashion!" He complied quickly, coming over me and between my thighs without losing his advantage. I aided him, but deprecatingly.

Once more he impatiently took up his divine movements. Now, being able to reach further within my sensitive sheath, his actions resulted so exquisitely that I felt compelled to second his motions. I laced my lithe thighs across his back and did so with a will. All my internal sources opened up to lubricate the path of his throbbing soul-prober.

Already I was on the verge of coming— when there was a knock on the door of my compartment—my companion ceased his divine administrations, his stiff engine almost dying of fright within me. Could it be my jealous German—trailing me—by any chance? The knocking became more insistent.

"*Qui est la?*" I asked fearfully.

"*L'inspecteur Suisse, madame. Pardon de vous deranger—mais votre passeeporte.*"

We were at the Swiss border. Greatly relieved, I told him that the car porter had my papers. He thanked me and moved on.

Mark was still within me—impotent with fright; but a few little squeezes of reminder from my well-controlled cunny soon brought him to. A few cooperative thrusts and he was back to proper pitch, and then he went at it again with redoubled vigor and zest, his member swelled more than ever as a result of the delay it had been subjected to.

The train had slowed down at the border; but was now picking up speed. Unconsciously my dear rider adopted the quickening tempo of the clattering wheels, compelling my own responsive heaves to be in kind. Soon we were at it at a furious rate, and our orgasm, a bit tardy because of its interruption, but all the more intense for the same reason, came on at last. I swooned with unbearable delight as, a moment later, he poured hot jets of his thick viscous love-balsam into my quivering receptacle, and lay upon me, overcome by delicious tremors, both of us simultaneously in the throes of that indescribable bliss which comes only when man and woman have together fulfilled (to all intents and purposes) their supreme biological function.

Exhausted now, not so much by love as by nights without rest, Mark slipped gently from my bosom and was immediately asleep. As for myself, sweet as was my languor, I lay awake almost an hour, revolving in my mind how I might aid the poor boy without hurting his pride. To give him money, even if unbeknownst to him, would make him feel as if he had been paid for the delight he had given me—and though I myself could accept money thus, as long as I could not afford to give away all of my love free, I had some regret for his no doubt more conventional standards. At last I hit upon it. At my destination I would write the University of Geneva and intercede for him. If necessary I would make some small endowment to the school. To anticipate: this was done successfully.

And now, about to settle down to sleep, something else occurred to me. My American friend had, in effect, taken a delicious advantage of me while I slept. What more poetic justice than to return the compliment in actuality?

Gently I removed the covers from off us and felt for his part. It lay curled up, peacefully soft upon him. I began to doubt the practicability of what I intended, since he was so deeply asleep. Changing my plans only partially however, I slipped noiselessly down lower in the bed until my head was opposite his middle, and carefully took his recumbent organ between my lips, stroking it very gently with my tongue. Immediately its blood began pulsating and it arose jerkily to approximate its former majesty. If I could get it stiff enough, I would climb stealthily over him, insert it in my ever-ready slot, and wake him with those same delicious rhythms that before had supposedly brought me from the Land of Nod to that of Prod. But due to his complete relaxation, as soon as I removed my lips, the organ began softening, and so I was compelled to resume my lingual titillations each time. Soon his light, regular breathing became more labored and intense, his hips made little thrusts as if performing some role in a dream, and before I had sucked upon his sensitive part scarcely a minute, a long flood of his delicious, glutinous love-sweets filled my mouth in slow spurts. He came thus quickly because of the utter lack of inhibitions during sleep. As my male readers know, the merest caress or pressure on their sex organs during sleep will generally suffice to bring on an immediate ejaculation accompanied by a pleasurable erotic dream.

With the climax, he began to stir and awaken; but before he had done so entirely, I was lying in my proper place beside him. In a whisper, he asked me whether I was awake. I replied that I was.

"I had the most wonderful dream about you just now," he said with the resonant voice of one just arisen refreshed from sleep. "I dreamt that you let me love you again. Only this time, you were upon me, our roles reversed . . ." and he went on to tell me all about it, little suspecting that his dream was the mere rationalization of a real enough stimulation, and that I had been the cause of it. Before many details of his picture had been sketched in, his John Henry was standing with interest. My own clitty, with that subtle sympathy that exists in all sensitive women, arose likewise to the occasion.

"How beautifully you describe your dream, Mark," I said. "You almost make me long to try it in actuality."

"Will you—please?" he begged eagerly.

I did not require much coaxing. In a moment I was above him, splitting my tender but willing cunt upon his now fully-wakened weapon. Fired by the lust that had been gathering in me from the moment I had first conceived my idea for raping his sleeping form down through my delicious sucking of him and through to this revised realization, I fucked him with a mad lubricity that before long had us both writhing in the pleasurable frenzy of approaching dissolution. What a heat my internal organs were in! What long luscious strokes I bestowed upon his member—and of course, my joyspot! When at last my wild, pumping cunt-suction brought on the delicious fruition of my efforts, his fervent discharge was as a cooling lotion to my steaming, fevered membranes. I ground down close to the root of the noble gland that coupled us, crushing our mounts together furiously, adding my own return to his—and then lay moaning and weeping upon his chest with unbearable pleasure.

But the best of things must end. As we lay in each other's embrace, the train pulled into a large, fully-lighted station. Mark peeped through the curtains. It was Geneva. Hurriedly he sprang into his clothes. There was but a twelve minute stop here. Quickly he kissed me again and again, and begged me to disclose my identity. I had to refuse, in order to preserve intact the sweet mystery of this adventure. "I know where to write you in case I can ever see you again," I told him, and with this he had to be contented. He left the train just as it started, and running alongside the moving car, waved me a long loving farewell from the cold deserted platform.

That was the last I ever saw of him, though I had the comfort of knowing that his desire to enter the University was indeed, through my efforts, realized.

# CHAPTER FOUR

At St. Moritz, I was met by my impatient friend—and we spent three delightful weeks together, engaging for that purpose two adjoining rooms at the hotel, of which the bed in one was considerably used. There were the winter sports, which brought the color to my cheeks in the crisp, tingling cold, and there was the indoor sports, which my lazy Spanish lover much preferred, and which brought the color to all of my body with their delicious heat.

After a morning's thrilling round of skiing and tobogganing, from which my companion would generally beg off, I rejoined him at the hotel for an afternoon of delicious intimacies. Our amorousness was perpetual, and to keep it from getting monotonous, my friend was of a most poetic and romantic temperament—besides which, he was never averse, as some men whom I have met are, to going down upon me for the celebration of those mystic rites brought to us from the Isle of Lesbos. And I was becoming myself quite a devotee of the lush Paphian method—which, added together, make sixty-nine.

"Your cunt, Madeleine," he would murmur from between my thighs, "is a beautiful scarlet flower in full bloom, and its perfumed recesses are ripe with the drippings of sweetest honey." And his lips would avidly seize upon the object of his adoration with such grateful pleasure that I would almost long to taste and kiss it myself—just to find out whether or not it was so much nicer than any others, as he told me so often. But having to satisfy myself with feasibilities, I would take his stiff tanned instrument between my lips and play upon it those exquisite tunes with which the auletrides of old used to charm their lovers. And of course, when finally he would favor my ardent mouth with the delicious proofs of his enjoyment, I would not think of insulting him and depriving myself of that dear essence of his virility.

Surely, one would think that some afternoons spent this way would soon satisfy even the most ardent woman. Yet, so increased by pleasures was my desire for pleasure, so ecstasy-provoking were my recollections of ecstasies just past—in brief, so incessant were my ever maturing passions becoming, that, if I were taking a warm bath alone, my finger would proceed at once to grant me the exquisite, slow, controlled relief that my pampered senses would not wait for otherwise, and that one would imagine I was the last woman in the world to have need of. And one morning, after as satisfying a night with my Hispanic lover as ever a woman could wish, I even went so far as to start a flirtation with a mysterious stranger in our skiing party. Without one word, he took my arm, and we skied off in a direction away from the crowd. Despite the thick falling snow, he led me direct to an emergency shelter on the mountain's ridge and silently laid me back upon the hard boards of the floor. As it was too cold to undress me, he deliberately ripped open a few inches of the inseam of my knickers with a tiny cigar-cutter, and through this narrow gun-slot proceeded to open fire upon the tender target. Throughout, no word was spoken by either of us. The silence of our meeting and our amorous combat made the eloquence of our gestures and motions all the more exquisite and keen. I wondered why he did not speak, but at the same time did not wish to break the peculiar spell that seemed to work so provocatively on both of us. The lambent flames that spread from my fiercely embattled fortress had thawed away the last trace of coldness from my body and sent titillating liquid fires racing through my veins —even then I suppressed my sighs and murmurs and made no sound. Only a soft, liquid, sucking sound could be heard, made by the slow withdrawal of his firm flesh from my moist sheath and its quick return. Outside the snow fell silently. Suddenly, without any heralding by loving words, his supreme crisis overtook him and his seed spurted maddeningly into my yet unsatisfied cunt. When he saw, however, from my continued upward thrusts that I had not yet had enough, he resumed his delicious fencing until I too surrendered the liquid tribute of my senses. But by this time, his own zest and libido rearoused, he stood his ground for another round of the tender, silent struggle, without withdrawing, and though I at first resented his thus taking advantage of a lady combatant already completely prostrated and helpless with pleasure, yet soon my own spirit of sportsmanship revived and we continued our wrestling give-and-take with full vigor until, this time better matched and timed, we both reached the ultimate divine discharge and collapsed together in a delicious "draw" that cast no reflections upon the fighting qualities of either of us.

When at last we arose, there were some white stains on my knickers, though scarcely noticeable because of the pepper and salt shade of the material. The stranger silently strapped on my skis for me, I pulled my sweater well below my hips to conceal the tear in the crotch, and we went out into the snow again—our bodies pulsatingly warm and invigorated by our quiet little interlude. We rejoined the party of skiers on a lower slope, where he left me without a word.

That very night, I saw him in the hotel lobby. I was in a quandary whether to recognize him or not. In a moment when I was alone he approached me. I had scarcely noticed his features during the morning, what with the blinding glare of the snow and then of my lubricity. But I saw now that he was a refined, handsome Frenchman.

"Madame must have concluded this morning that I was devoid of the power of speech. But no. Words obscure the true passions of the flesh and vitiate the ardent perfumes of desire. If I had spoken, it would have been to say 'I love you,' and yet who knows what 'love' means? How could I guess what connotations or qualifications, perhaps unpleasant, perhaps foolishly sentimental or conventional, you might attach to your conception of the word? The phrase is better left unsaid, though the gods know that what I felt toward you as a beautiful woman offering the divine gift of herself was, if not love, something no whit inferior to it."

I was enthralled by the delicate precision of his speech.

"You have read Remy de Gourmont, madame?" he went on. Of course I had, this writer's books constituting, as they well deserve to, the very Bible of all sensualists. I nodded.

"Well, like him, I love passion for itself. What need is there then to encumber it with base justifications, to obscure its iridescent colors and heady perfumes and exquisite tones, already ineffable beyond words, with a cloud of metaphysics? As he says, I love passion for itself, for that which it brings with it of movement, life, immediate sensation. And what sensation, pray, is more immediate, more genuine, more completely and directly experienced than that of love? To touch something exquisite, that is to experience a sensation emanating from something outside things, even to perform a motion that is pleasing to the muscles, all these things are similar. But to love—ah, that is all of these things combined, plus something that transcends them all—that sensation originating within that does not submit to the measurement of any of the senses and hence defines all words."

I was fascinated.

"I would much like to meet you again," he said. "Only in more civilized circumstances than the last. I do not often, I assure you, embrace fully-clothed women."

I arranged to join him in his room the very next morning, pretending to my lie-abed Spaniard to be out tobogganing—and we had two hours of the most delicious and prolonged epicurean connection I have ever experienced. With a peculiarly subtle intuition he would slow down and stop just as he or I was approaching the climax, which, delightful though it be, is alas the end and not the beginning of pleasure. By thus stopping short we were able to slowly savor the delicious sensation in all of its varying shades just this side of the dissolution. With uncanny insight and deftness he would add a timely stroke now and then to keep the exquisite feeling from fading, or would grind into me with a rotating movement that increased the frenzy of my steaming wet cunny without actually bringing on the end. His control was marvelous. For an hour he kept this up, till we were both bathed in inexpressible bliss, and, despite our pact of silence I was writhing about with the unbearable burning ecstasies, uttering cries and moans for more, for relief, thrashing my arms about, my fevered head falling from side to side—while he rode firmly upon me, flushed with pleasure and with the triumph of killing me with joy. At last I could stand it no more—his prolonged teasing had me in a delirium—my heart seemed to be bursting with the excessive pleasure.

"Please—Andre—finish me—for God's sake!" I gasped. "Oh—please—you will kill me!"

Seeming to comply, he favored me with four or five furiously fast, delicious strokes that carried me on toward that deeply-needed conclusion. But then suddenly—oh how I hated him at the time and how I loved him for it afterward—just as I felt but one more stroke was needed to bring me down from that high precipice whose rarified atmosphere I could no longer endure, he stopped short as if equipped with four-wheel brakes, arresting the progress of my sensation at an intense pitch most unbearable of all.

I cried, I moaned, I begged. With all my power I tried by my own efforts to bring on the delicious climax; but he pinned me down with his greater strength and rotated his stiff teasing member within me in a reverse direction, stimulating me to further frenzy, though not in the required manner.

I screamed out. Another such deceit and I would faint away. Andre brought his mouth to mine and took possession of my burning lips in a long exquisite kiss that soothed me somehow by momentarily diverting my senses from my cunny. Our hot breaths intermingled, our souls dissolved together. Holding me thus, his strong loins withdrew the full length of his swimming, lust-maddened sheath with exquisite slowness—repeated the motion a second time without haste. Every step of the intensification of my pleasure passed like a slow cinema before my consciousness. A third, a fourth, a fifth! Oh gods! The dangerous peak of supreme agonizing pleasure is at hand! If he forsakes me now, I perish without doubt. But no! Another slow withdrawal that clamped my throat, intercepted my breath, and bade my heart stop beating while my cunny should decide my suspended fate—and he plunges home to the hilt, hurling me down at last toward the swift-flowing river of pleasure below that breaks the fall from the great etherian heights of the climax. Nor does he leave things to nature even now, but with lightning-like rapid short strokes follows up and intensifies my delicious dissolution and brings on his own. Oh what exquisite relief! I shuddered, I twitched in the overpowering grip of pleasure as he shot into my already-flooded cunt a stinging, scalding load of his long-frustrated thick, boiling sperm. For ten minutes thereafter I was completely hysterical. My lips, my breasts, and of course my cunny, were so supersensitive that any touch made me laugh and cry at the same time like an idiot. But it was a delicious hysteria, dear reader, and I would wish each one of you right now no worse than a similar experience.

As we rested from our labors of love, Andre broke the silence for the first time.

"How voluptuous your figure is, Madeleine," he said, "and voluptuousness alone is the quality that constitutes beauty—for to me beauty is no more than the promise of pleasure. And your body, every fold and nook and cranny, every smooth surface—and all of it is finest alabaster—is meant only to give pleasure to men. Even your darling foot—" he bent to kiss my instep—"is as of genuine mother of pearl. What god would spurn to have you thrill him with that perfect little foot of yours?" And intrigued with the idea, he had me stroke for a while his already stiff and upstanding love-organ with the soft sole of my foot. With similar compliments I was induced to let him sample the possible pleasures of all the rest of my body: in the soft cup formed by the crook of my knee, in the rich folds that bordered my cunny, on the satiny surface of my belly, immediately over the depression of my navel, between the tender yielding mounds of my breasts, beneath my warm silk-lined armpits. Nor did I deny him a tiny caress with my full mouth and lips—

even from the silken tresses of my hair, garlanded about his sensitive phallus, he showed me how he could derive pleasure; and of course, there was the deep delicious groove between my plump buttocks, even apart from the tight, cozy sheath it led into. In none of these places did he spend—only, as he told me, before he could even begin to tire of me, he would have to try them all. Hence I was assured of his ardent friendship for at least the balance of my little vacation.

After toying with me in my nudity awhile, he insisted that I don my transparent chemise of pale green chiffon. "To look at your white body too long is like looking at the sun," he said, "and anyway, art prefers that nude women should be adorned with some article of clothing to relieve the purity and frankness of their outlines—even if only a girdle or silk stockings—to accentuate the nudity by demarking it—or a diaphanous veil or chemise to add piquancy, suggestiveness or mystery, to challenge the imagination and the keenness of vision."

"Who are you here with?" he suddenly asked me for the first time. "Your husband?"

"No," I replied. "He is just my . . . my. . ."

"Oh, that doesn't matter," he relieved me. "I am a writer. You are a beautiful woman. It is not disgraceful for a man to live by his intelligence, nor for a woman to live by her beauty. With woman's inherent generosity you give yourself when you can, you sell yourself when you must." He brought out one of my full breasts from under the bodice of my chemise and nibbled tentatively, then exquistely on the scarlet bud that crowned it.

"A lover . . . no doubt one who has much greater claims upon you than I, and yet I have no compunctions about borrowing the use of your delicious form. Isn't it de Gourmont again who says, 'Women, like hedge flowers, belong to those who gather them'? Like hedges they may grow on the edge of someone's private property, but like the flowers that blossom on these hedges and overhang the public domain, they belong by common law to whosoever gathers them. Women, things of rare beauty, must be dedicated to the public. I can no more countenance a really beautiful woman belonging to one man who keeps her jealously and exclusively to himself than I could endure to have the Sistine Chapel guarded by watchdogs or the Julier-Pitz out there that so entrances our view and invites us to climb and explore her white heights, to be surrounded by a barbed fence. Even the most desirable woman or object will be ultimately tired of by any man who too repeatedly sates himself therewith. Is its beauty henceforth to be completely wasted by too strict a regard for the laws of property engendered by the impotent?"

In such a fine vein did Andre continue, giving certainty and sustenance to the principles that guided my life. When at last he lapsed into silence to once more give all his senses to the worship of my body, which now burned to be possessed by this man who understood and appreciated it so exquisitely, I gave all of myself—making him promise only that he would not repeat his divine excessive teasing twice in the same morning. The approach of luncheon forbade too prolonged a connection anyway.

This time, he had me lie on my side with my back to him, my upper thigh raised and resting on his. From this position he inserted his dear self in the moist, well-padded slit that is as accessible from the rear as from the front, if not more so, and slowly pushing it to the hilt, allowed me to bring my thighs together. Holding me close to him, his arms about my waist, his belly pressed pleasantly against my posteriors, he had me bend my trunk forward at right angles to himself, the better to facilitate his movements within me and to bring my clitty in direct contact with his bar. In this snug posterior-lateral position, my cunt was able to engulf even more of him than in the front method, the moist downy lips kissing his very love purse—and more important still, since he was not upon me, I had as much freedom of movement as he.

Back and forth we both moved in unison, pressing toward each other together, separating together, his superb ivory pillar forcing its way through the moist resilient folds of my sheath, now so tightly clasped about him by reason of my legs being held together that a most audible and sensible vacuum was created with each luscious withdrawal of his firm piston. At the same time his hot hands wandered wantonly over the whole front and back of my body and thighs, pressing my soft elastic breasts, my belly, my mount, and the snowy elevations of my buttocks that were placed so conveniently to his reach, at last coming to rest over the essential garden of delight with a finger slipped between the downy portieres to pay additional court to my excited joy-spot.

Oh, the inexpressible happy delight of our rhythmic unencumbered body heavings! Oh, the incomparable bliss of drawing the hot moist flesh of my now-fiery cavern over the full length of his satin-textured weapon and sitting back on it again, letting it sink into me to the very handle, getting the utmost out of his exquisite dilatation.

Soon the approaching climax spurred us both on to an even more voluptuous abandon. The fast friction of his prick, its whole length traversed in double-quick time by our joint efforts, sent flaming tongues of titillating sensation up my abdomen and spine, his deft finger caressing my masterful little protuberance at such moments as it came away from its stroker, making it additionally certain that the gathering intensity of sensation should not lapse for the fraction of a second.

Panting and sobbing, I hurried on to my climax, aided in every way by my strong, silent lover. At last—what joy! The supreme convulsion burst upon me, blinding me, dazzling me with its intensity. My womb contracted sharply, squeezing the liquid secretions into my quivering channel. All my glands gave up the last drop of their contents. It was like a delicious bleeding to death—and indeed, I nearly died of the blissful pain. Back into his lap I pressed with a madly oscillating movement, my cunny grasping his flesh convulsively in the desperation of its overpowering, agonized pleasure. I turned my head over my shoulder and met his hot mouth in a long kiss that completed the circuit of electrifying sensations that flowed through our bodies. His hands each took to themselves a full heaving breast—and with one final thrust that threatened to crash through my whole writhing body he poured his burning blissful treasure into my quivering cunt, mingling our loving effusions in a sweet balm that soothed and extinguished the still fitful fires that flared in that part. Through my kisses I uttered little gasping cries of joy. He strained me close, close, close to his dear body, and here we swooned away with pleasurable relief.

Was I exhausted by this morning of delicious amorous combat, dear reader? I was not. After a bath and a hearty luncheon, I joined my Spaniard full of desire for a recontinuation of the morning's delights.

All in all, as you may gather, I spent a most enjoyable time in Switzerland.

# CHAPTER FIVE

Back to Paris again. I must now pass quickly over a period of years. By now I have given the indulgent reader a fairly representative account of how my days and nights were spent. My escapades, interesting and thrilling as they all were in actuality, would in writing seem but tiresome repetitions.

During this time I extended the circle of my acquaintances and lovers to include many fascinating literary and artistic denizens of the Left Bank, though all in all I still adhered to diplomats and financiers as being far more remunerative. It was not long before Fleurette alone was insufficient to take care of all my cast-off lovers. It was then that a close and critical search of the city discovered pretty brunette Manon who was added to my staff, and who only recently left my service to marry a wealthy English manufacturer whom she met through me. Before long a third, Suzanne, joined my forces. At this time, I must have it understood, I was not operating a "house." Except Fleurette, who lived with me, Manon and Suzanne had separate apartments, and our cooperation was merely social. We would meet frequently and I would contrive to put lovers within range of their charms, but beyond that our association was secret.

It was in 1923, I believe, over three years after I left New York, that my next great adventure took place. It came about this way. Count B——, a Russian diplomat, had been madly infatuated with me. An unfortunate, though not unusual, arrangement of circumstances had kept him for a long time from getting to my bedside. When at last the obstacle was disposed of and he was just about to attain my embraces, an even more unfortunate circumstance arose: he was recalled to Petrograd by his Imperial Government. Distracted by this added stroke of ill fortune, the count threatened everything from suicide to disobeying his Tzar's orders and remaining with me. As at the time I had been contemplating a tour of Eastern Europe, I saved the day by offering to accompany him if he would return. He was overjoyed. Thus it was that I came to spend some months in the Russian capital.

The two days' traveling on the train, needless to say, was an almost uninterrupted round of fucking. The atmosphere of our private compartment was actually musky with the heavy odors of perfumes and of repeated seminal discharges, and its stimulation alone was enough to bring us back to venereal delights again and again.

The Russian capital, when we arrived there, was not in a very festive state. So far as royal entertainment was concerned, there was none. The Tzar himself, a haughty, sullen and suspicious nincompoop, was almost impossible to meet. Like every other wearer of the Russian purple, his sole concern, apart from his private vices, was the dodging of imaginary bombs and the extirpation of all free thought minorities. The Tzaritza, an attractive enough piece from the glimpse I caught of her once, was a similar snob. As the count told me, ever since her affair with General Orlov (the undoubted real father of the little crown prince) had leaked out, she did not dare to appear in public.

All our social contacts then were made through the few salons we visited, such as that of Prince Andronnikov. Here I met most of the really important figures in Russian politics. The unpopularity of the Tzaritza was unanimous, and the favorite topic of scandal was her brazen goings-on with the dissolute monk Rasputin, who seemed to be the real man of the hour and the man behind the Russian throne. Madame Alexandar von Pistolkors, the sister of the Tzaritza's lady-in-waiting, who became quite a good friend of mine, told me that she had it from the monk himself (who had no compunctions about bragging of his royal connections) that the Empress of all the Russias would devoutly spread her thighs for him at any time. And what's more, so completely did the monk have the Tzar under his thumb that the latter would have to stand by and like it. Whether all this was the truth or merely malicious scandal, I could not judge at the time. But I could not help but become interested in this strange figure of Rasputin, the crude Russian muzhik who controlled a nation, to whom all sorts of strange hypnotic powers were attributed, and of whom it was said that the most beautiful and desirable women in all the land would travel thousands of miles, trade away their jewels and betray their husbands to spend one night with him . . . although it was also said that he was so fed up with the adulation of princesses and countesses that he showed a marked preference for actresses, courtesans and foreign

**women.** I could not consider leaving Russia without meeting, by any means possible, this unusual character.

The closest I could come to him for some time, however, was some weeks later, when I induced a young revolutionary student whom I had met informally at the public art gallery in Petersburg, to take me to hear the monk deliver a sermon at one of the churches in the lower part of the city. It was a snowy night, and as we rode across town in a hired "dorshky," Alexei, who was a peculiar feverish sort of a fellow whom I could not fathom at all, sat silently wrapped in his great fur coat at the opposite end of the seat, paying not the least heed to my coquettish attentions. He was frankly anarchistic and hated the Russian Orthodox Church bitterly, so our excursion was scarcely to his taste, and it had been by dint of considerable coaxing that I had induced him to undertake it at all.

The church was a gloomy edifice dating no doubt from the Middle Ages. Situated though it was in a poor quarter of the town, there were, much to my surprise, among the miserable congregation a great number of richly gowned and bejeweled ladies who seemed to be waiting with great expectancy, similar to mine, the advent of the great and holy Rasputin.

At last, heralded by shouts of admiration and awe, the great man appeared in the pulpit. I recognized him at once from the many descriptions I had received. He wore a long black craftan and was fully bearded; but his face was remarkably sweet, youthful and disarming.

Proceeding to bless the assembly, everyone fell to their knees. I was about to follow suit, in accordance with the adage of how one acts when in Rome, but was restrained by the example of Alexei, who remained standing beside me. As the gaze of the holy monk wandered over the heads of the hundreds kneeling, he discovered us two standing defiantly. Instantly his face darkened demoniacally, his forehead furrowed by a deep frown, and his strange pale blue eyes glittered violently. A moment later, though, noting that one of the sinners was an attractive woman, his face lighted up again and he favored me with an insolent lickerish leer, even as he spoke the words of his benediction. In those few moments the whole multiplicity of the man's aspect was disclosed to me. First, the sincere, kindly peasant-preacher, then the baleful, vengeful antagonist, and finally and above all, the lewd lascivious libertine to whom women were far greater a concern than God.

He went on with his sermon while all listened attentively. His voice was rich, soothing and caressing; but beneath its unctuousness there was a suggestion of sneering irony which, to the unblinded listener, proclaimed that he was himself above believing the nonsense he preached. As he spoke slowly and simply, I had no great difficulty following his Russian, though now and then I had to call upon Alexei to interpret an unfamiliar word or expression.

Only through repentance and humility could salvation be attained, he told us. But how can one sincerely repent if one has not first sinned? Virtue itself brings arrogance, and the arrogant cannot win heaven. Only through sin can one drive out evil, fighting fire with fire. So long as you bear sinful desires secretly within you, you are a hypocrite and odious to the Lord. So out with the desires. Sin and have done with it! (A splendid piece of sophistry which meant in effect: "It is sinful to want to fuck; but the only way to stop wanting it is to do it." In a flash I saw the reason for his tremendous popularity. People —ignorant women especially—have always wanted a moral justification for their carnal lusts. It would not do to come right out and admit fucking is divine—oh no—that would be against the Bible. But ah—to say that fucking is filthy and sinful, but it's divine to get that sin out of your system—that's religion.)

After his brief but enthusiastically received sermon, all joined in the singing of weird hymns and folk songs, during which the monk circulated among the crowd, touching the women here and there with gestures whose sanctimoniousness could scarcely conceal their lasciviousness. Usually he contented himself with touching merely their shoulders or their foreheads; but sometimes he would "heal their hearts" by stroking the full breast that intervened. It was a great racket to get away with in the name of God; but monks have, under the auspices of the Almighty, done far worse things than "feel" women.

With the distribution of his caresses, the singing became more enlivened; then there was dancing, wild and abandoned, the monk himself participating. The religious fever—or mob fury, to designate it more honestly—kept mounting higher and higher. It was almost as bad as a Holy Roller meeting back in the good old civilized United States. Before long, frantic, hysterical women, who could not all share in the embraces of the holy monk, threw themselves into the arms of strange men—who, nothing loathe, and their senses similarly whipped up by this exquisite religion, were soon ripping open well-filled bodices and raising skirts, uncovering monstrous Tartar pricks and shoving their "devils" into hells where they proceeded with lust-maddened motions to rid themselves of their burdens of sin and attain the ecstasy of repentance. I could scarcely believe my eyes. Two "politzia" entered to investigate the uproar. A gesture from the monk and they left immediately. So contagious indeed was the spirit of the mad orgy that even my own heart began beating excitedly—and Alexei, carried away, put his hand into my bosom amorously and crushed me meaningfully close to him. "Not here!" I whispered. "Later, if you must." He accepted the postponement. A moment after, a strange, panting, red-faced Russian pounced upon me and proceeded without ado to lay me onto a bench. Alexei struck him a strong blow behind the ear that felled him like an ox—and gathering me up, dragged me out of the turbulent mob. Back at my hotel, I did not violate my promise. Alexei came up to my suite with me. Lying at my feet on a fur hearth-rug before a roaring log fire, he began for the first time making love to me. I had changed into a light, flowing negligee of a diaphanous material which, as I passed before the fire, had permitted the full silhouette of my form to be glimpsed.

"You are so majestically beautiful, dorogoh (dear) Madeleine!" he murmured, embracing my knees. "You are like a queen—so cold and unapproachable in your beauty." Cold and unapproachable! When I was just dying for him to hurry and get started. . . . "I would give my life now, merely to kiss you —but to even raise myself to the level of your lips would seem a sacrilege, so far above me are you, my divinity!"

"But Alexei," I protested, "I am not a god hungry for companionship—for love even. . ."

"You do not understand, dear Madeleine," he spoke moodily. "Your sunny Western temperament cannot fathom the dark abysses of the Russian soul. We are an accursed people —a nation of cruelly mistreated slaves. My bitterness, my moroseness comes from the brooding melancholy of long winter days and nights behind the stove, spent in soul-clawing introspection, in impotent raging against injustices of every sort." He paused and gazed into the fire. From the ballroom of the hotel below could be heard strains from one of Tchaikowsky's symphonies, played by a moody balaleika orchestra, its gloomy music telling of perpetual snow over the Siberian steppes, of an old man weeping over the corpse of his son, just struck down by the Tzar's cruel cossacks, while the snow falls and falls. . .

"We Russians are an abnormal people," he went on, breaking into my revery. "It comes from too frequent use of the 'knout.' The Tzar, accursed be his name, beats his ministers; the ministers beat their subordinates; officers beat their soldiers, and soldiers beat the populace. My father always whipped my mother at the slightest pretext, or with none at all, both of them would whip *me*. Only I had no one to abuse in turn, and I had to endure—and in time learned to like it. I loved my mother for her cruelty; yet I hated my father for his. Perhaps it was because he beat her, too. When, while I was yet but fifteen years old, he was shot down by the Tzar's soldiers in some peasant uprising, I was so happy that I got drunk and remained away from home for over three nights.. Later, mother, who was still young and attractive— she had married when scarcely twelve, as is the barbaric practice among us—would let me, her only child, sleep with her. She meant no harm—Russian nights are cold—and we were too poor to heat our room—but my thoughts became incestuously lustful. As she slept, I would more and more boldly caress and investigate her soft female form. Maddened by prurient desires I would try to satisfy myself with my hand, imagining myself in possession of that delicious body whence I came. One night, when in my furtive caresses, I had dared to stroke her widowed sex parts, she suddenly awoke, took me fiercely in her arms, and bursting into tears, told me she had just had a wonderful dream of father . . . You don't mind my telling you all this, do you, dear Madeleine?"

"Oh no, Alexei," I said, stroking his hair with tender encouragement. In truth, I was considerably aroused by his lewd, incestuous picture. If most of my readers find the idea repulsive, I must opine bluntly that it is for the reason that most of our parents are too elderly to be sexually attractive to us. His, as the case of the mother of Baudelaire, was obviously an exception. He went on.

"At last, one night, unable to contain myself further, I raped the sleeping form of my mother. She awoke. She protested. But I know she enjoyed it too. When finally I threw my burning seed into her womb—the same womb that sheltered me in my gestation—the fierce joy of executing this criminally proscribed act of incest was so great that I knew from that moment that no other woman could ever give me a comparable pleasure. As I thus desecrated the body of this woman whose sole misfortune was to be both my genetrix and a beautiful, desirable woman besides, it seemed that once and for all I was avenging the suffering her husband, my father, had inflicted upon me.

"When at length she broke from my boyish but brutal embrace, she was furious with shame and remorse—and leaving the bed, fetched immediately the very 'knout' that father had so often used on us. With this cruel instrument she vented upon me all her moral indignation, whipping me with all her strength upon my bare body. But as the stinging thongs of the leather cut across my flesh, I experienced only a divine, martyred pleasure. With every stroke I loved that woman more and more. The orgasm which I had scarcely had time to finish upon her soft, white body, now resumed, as was evidenced by the repeated liquid phenomenon at my parts. I fainted away in torment and rapture, and my mother, exhausted by her efforts, desisted and carried me back to bed, comforting me with her kisses and caresses, weeping and begging me to forgive her. Slyly I took advantage of her present state, and soon I was within her again, committing once more the delicious crime against nature—this time with her full cooperation. It was not long before I had established my right to this incestuous connection at will, only always I would insist that she whip me before its consummation. Oh, if you could only imagine the delight of being maltreated by a woman whom one loves, the tormenting bliss of being her complete slave, her plaything, subject to her every whim—to be beaten fiercely and then perhaps to be taken back into her forgiving arms for a moment. . .

"Mother is dead to me now. Betraying doubly our own delicious relationship—perhaps her sense of sin conquered after all—she married a wealthy landowner scarcely a year after father's demise—and I was sent away to school. During my military service, I would frequently violate some trifling regulation solely for the pleasure of being reprimanded, or better still, cuffed or whipped. Much as my mind and pride would resent the punishment, my body would tingle and glow in a strange way. I would suffer pain, but I would enjoy it."

He fell silent again. I continued fondling his hair, a little awed by the amazing intricacy of the man's character—a little impatient, too, at his seeming obliviousness of me. But no, it was only to make himself better understood before he could love me—for now he again began caressing my legs, murmuring words of endearment, of worship and self-debasement.

"I want to be your slave, oh gorgeous Madeleine. Here, in token of my vanquishment, I place my neck beneath your tiny foot." He did so. "Now, kick me—spurn me—only let me be your slave. I will execute the most menial tasks you can find for me. Reward me only with blows. But let me belong to you—let me be near you always."

"Alexei!" I spoke sharply. "Put an end to all this talk of slavery and mistreatment. You are my equal—if you were not, I would not have you here. We are not living in the days of Roman autocrats, with slaves over whom we have the right of life or death!"

"Alas that we are not!" he went on. "That is why my life is so miserable and unfulfilled. I have sought everywhere a woman who would love me a little and chastise me often. But in Russia, the women themselves wish to be beaten and cannot be induced to lift the knout. Oh mother, mother!"

For a time we were both silent. Alexei, completely prostrated at my feet and gazing up at me from the rug with a mad, worshipful humility, deigned only to remove my slippers and kiss my bare toes, running his burning cheeks across the cool soles of my feet. Sympathetic as I felt for his malady I could not quite reconcile his avowed slavishness with the role of a man.

I lost patience with him. In wrestling my foot from his embrace I kicked him. His eyes lit up almost ecstatically as he gazed into my now flushed, angry face.

"Ah, what a beautiful, what a cruel tyrant you would make! And how I would love you!"

"Alexei! You ought to have your foolish delusions beaten out of you! You deserve to be whipped!"

"Whipped?" He sprang to his feet eagerly. From his fur coat he fetched a long heavy whip, a knout, I presume—the symbol of Russian autocracy. He laid it upon my lap, and divesting himself of his shirt in a moment, threw himself once more at my feet.

"Now!" he whispered hoarsely, "my goddess! Whip me! Kill me! To see your eyes flash again—to feel your wrath—oh, beat me, please!"

I fingered the whip fearfully. Its thongs were heavy and knotted. In a civilized country it would not be used even on a horse. I shuddered.

"Alexei," I said, "I forgive you without a whipping. Delude yourself no more with these base fantasies. You can stay with me tonight. And look—I am all yours, to love me as you will." I opened my negligee and offered my nude body temptingly.

He shut his eyes with insane resolution. "I cannot love you," he said, "unless you torture me first. You are an indifferent stranger to me if you will not accept my slavery and establish your right to my body by the knout."

"Can't there be love without suffering?" I pleaded. "Pleasure without pain? That alone is my ideal, and I think—am I not correct? —that it was attained by the Greeks."

"That was before Christianity. Now all pleasure is sin, is inextricably bound up with the idea of transgression, humility and pain. In childhood we are taught to love a cruel God, to accept his myriad afflictions and adversities as so many blessings, as marks of his deep concern and love for us. Now that I have no God, I must still love cruelty. Political tyranny I am, alas, too enlightened to accept. But in the tyranny of a beautiful woman there is nothing inconsonant with my ideas —and it would satisfy that deep inescapable craving within me. One of the sexes must dominate, and to my mind, women are the destined rulers. Without the quotation of biological and anthropological authority, suffice it to say that they are the mothers and molders of the race. To them men are but a temporary means to an end. It is for them to give or withhold their cold, beautiful selves, to curb the mad, fruitless lusts of men and control the destiny of nations. Yes, as Sacher-Masoch says, since it is the woman who is always the one desired, through his passions Nature has given man over into woman's hands."

"But Alexei," I protested, "that is entirely fallacious. It overlooks the fact that women may desire men as strongly as men desire women. Your and Masoch's experience with the perhaps cold women of the North may have forced you to such a conclusion; but you are wrong, I tell you, you are wrong. Take the women of my France, or of Spain or Italy. They are, if anything, more amorous than the men. Why, more, they may even desire to be dominated by men in the very manner you crave of women. The same

101

repression that makes you mystify and exaggerate the majesty of women would make the women feel likewise toward men. Only I do believe that women are closer to Nature, less blinded by too much reflection, and hence less addicted to fantasies such as yours. But why can't you take life as it is, Alexei? Why can't you accept me as an equal?"

"I can't," he groaned. "There are no equals in Russia. Everyone preys or is preyed upon. But why do we talk? Beat me . . ."

"No, Alexei," I said, "I couldn't. I am not Russian."

We were silent. He lay at my feet, like a dog—only unlike even a dog, he begged for punishment. It was getting late. I arose. "I must retire now, Alexei," I said. "I am sorry for you, but I do not twice offer myself to the same man—or any man. You may go." He clung to my feet. "You may go Alexei," I pronounced firmly. He made no move, other than to kiss my feet passionately.

"You may go, Alexei!" I repeated for the third time, exasperated, and with menace in my voice; but he clung to me more desperately than ever. I was genuinely angered. And granting his point of view theoretically as much as I would, I still could not endure the actuality of his abjectness. What sort of game was he playing with me? I had offered myself and he, like a worm, had refused me. Perhaps a little taste of the medicine he begged for would soon convince him that blows are not so sweet as kisses . . .

I picked up the knout. Its weight, its pliancy, its whole unaccustomed feel—gave to my arm a strange sense of power.

"Will you go, Alexei?" I asked for the last time.

"Beat me, kill me, dearest woman!" he cried, "but do not force me to leave your divine presence!"

Enough! Through the air I swung the whip. . . and brought it down upon his bare back. The leather snapped about his shoulders, leaving a scarlet line across his dark skin. That should do for him, I thought, but he made no move to go or to plead for mercy. I struck him again—more vigorously. Stubbornly, he made no sound. Once more I brought the knout down upon him—with all my strength. I would make him relent! Again and again I struck him, till his back was a crisscross of red welts. If he had said one word. I would have gladly desisted; but his obstinacy aroused undreamt-of powers of cruelty within me. Since it fazed him so little, it *was* a quite exhilarating sport, this whip swinging—and I was becoming momenttarily more expert at it. I was soon breathless and flushed with my cruel exertions.

"Remove the rest of your clothes, Alexei!" I commanded. I was determined to give him the supreme whipping of his life. He complied, and in a minute lay on the floor with his entire back nude to me. I resumed with vicious strength, striking now his thighs and buttocks. Only by breaking his will could I reestablish my self-respect. I lashed with all the force and swing in my body, furiously discarding my negligee when its flimsy stuff hampered my movements. My breasts, my whole form vibrated vigorously. I was the very incarnation of fury—and every moment increased the brutality of my passion. Now, impatient even of the time required to draw back the whip for each blow, I struck back and forth from side to side, getting in two blows for every one before.

Soon there was no inch of his back that I had not marked with the writing of my hatred.

"Have you had enough now, dog?" I panted. He made no reply. With my foot I turned his body upward. Tears were streaming from his eyes, but his expression was ecstatic and martyred. "More," he whispered. "Divine woman, I will crawl after you through the public streets, your slave! More!"

More! Were all my efforts indeed nothing to him so far? Murderously, insanely, I redoubled my blows—striking till I could strike no more—upon his head, his face, anywhere. At last, exhausted, I sank upon the rug beside him. A thin stream of blood ran from his lip, where I had struck too blindly. The sight caused me suddenly to be overcome by remorse. I took him into the soft shelter of my arms and kissed him. For the first time he was responsive and hugged me tenderly.

All emotions are fomented by similar chemical forces. My blood was heated by the violence of my exercise. Imperceptibly almost, my boiling hatred changed to burning desire. Alexei must have been similarly affected, for his love organ now stood out erect and stiff from his pain-striped body.

"Forgive me, Alexei," I murmured passionately. "Forgive me! What can I do to make amends for my cruelty?"

"I want you . . . now!" he said tensely; but too weak perhaps, he made no move to come upon me. "Love me," he whispered, "I am your slave. Use me—then trample me under foot again."

My lasciviousness was too much aroused, my desire too far gone for me to stop at nice details. Panting with urgent lust I straddled his body and eagerly spitted my hot swimming cunt upon his upstanding part, slowly sinking down upon it till I had engulfed it to the hilt, till his reservoirs of love pressed close against my buttocks and perineum. Even as I sat for a moment in this delicious position, I could feel his member swelling further within me, giving me that incomparably exquisite well-filled sensation that comes only when one's warm sensitive sheath fits its dear cylindrical visitor like a tight glove. With what hungry delight I relished the superb impalement! Slowly I raised my crouching body, my feet upon the floor, my hands supporting me against his ribs, until all but the very head of his turgid instrument had left my hot humid nest; then, quickly and with a single continuous motion sitting down upon it again, I felt his hard smooth flesh flow over my soft clinging membranes till it penetrated to the utmost within my quivering belly. I pressed down upon him with all my might, till I could feel his stiff shaft distending the uppermost end of my hungry vagina, clamoring for entrance into my very womb.

Now, panting with hot desire, I began my movements in deadly earnest, rising up and then plunging down and around, caressing his bursting organ with the subtle spiral strokes of my clasping cunny. Electrified with pleasure at last, my pain-loving masochistic companion, so divinely linked to my hot flesh, pressed up to meet my thrusts while his hands reached out to fondle and mold my palpitating breasts. But alas, this exquisite connection was too good to last! Already worked up close to the melting point of his flagellation at my hands, a few of my delicious pumping strokes was all that he could stand. Seizing my buttocks fiercely to intensify our close conjunction, he suddenly yielded to his climax with a low cry, shooting upward into my pulsating body a spurting generous flood of his hot tantalizing seed.

I rolled and heaved desperately upon him to bring on my own highest pleasure, but his vigor was not up to the task. As my efforts, with the subsidence of his essential medium, became less and less availing, my urgent desire gave way to angry disappointment. Coming from off his futile impotent body and standing beside him, I kicked his still quivering prostrate form with vicious exasperation. After all these hours of dawdling and exertion, after fulfilling his every desire, here was I, completely stranded and unsatisfied.

I took up the whip again. Perhaps a few cuts of the knout would make him useful again. But no, it was unavailing. I had pumped him dry—all too well.

Slipping into my negligee again, I seated myself on the fauteuil by the fireplace—a most inauspicious place to cool my fevered senses. A malicious idea came to me.

"Alexei!" I said, "come over here." Painfully, with humility, he dragged his nude, tortured body over the floor to my feet. Opening my negligee in front, I spread my knees apart. My cunny was still dripping the generous results of his consummation.

"Alexei, I want you to thrill me with your lips—with your mouth and with your tongue."

He looked up in horor.

"But madame—you may practice that vice in your France, but here in Russia, it is unheard of! Wives may be forced to do the equivalent to their husbands, but for a man to do it to a woman—oh no! Command anything, but not that!"

His evident and declared repugnance made me all the more determined to have him do it. The very element of compulsion would give me an added lascivious pleasure—as if I were a man, cruelly raping and defiling a young and unwilling girl. I reached for the whip and struck him brutally across the shoulder with its heavy butt.

"You miserable, ungrateful wretch!" I hissed, taxing my Russian vocabulary to the utmost. "You disgusting, detestable pervert, you—you will balk at what I ask you, after I have satisfied your own base cravings!" I punctuated each epithet with a blow of the knout. Never before in my life had I felt so majestically, so ruthlessly cruel.

In his eyes pride struggled with abject slavish admiration. I dropped the whip and sent my hand out in a stinging slap across his cheek. Thus does power become assured and arrogant when it is undisputed. Tangling my fingers in his thick disheveled hair, I dragged his head up to the level of my thighs, and then with both my hands forced his face against my spew-bathed cunt.

"Now slave!" I screamed hysterically, "wallow in your own vile exudations! Drink up that essence of your detestable self which you dared to defile me with!" And locking my soft thighs tightly about his neck, I viciously rubbed my dripping furrow over his whole face, as one would punish a fouling dog, bringing my most sensitive parts against his lips. For a time he remained thus, doing nothing, —only his frame seemed to be shaken by deep sobs. But in my passionate lust I was far beyond pitying him. Furiously I punched and pulled at his head.

"Your tongue! Lick! Lap! Suck! You hound!"

Reluctantly, gingerly, his tongue came out and felt timidly the upper part of my slit. Impatient with his hesitancy, however, I forced him down to the deepest, wettest part of the groove—to accustom him all at once. Soon he was following the directions that I gasped to him, now licking up and down, now across, now stopping his tongue to suck the erect hypersensitive clitty at my command.

Soon the delirious climax approached. I was blind with the fury of my passion, panting, writhing, as I crushed his mouth, his whole face, into my turbulent center.

"Now quickly! More quickly! More! More, or I'll kill you!" I cried.

The supreme orgasm burst upon me in a sadistic frenzy of pleasurable agony. My thighs were locked rigidly about his head and as the waves of sensation convulsed my whole body I beat and tore at the agent of my delirium. The same rending delights that ordinarily express the supreme intensification of love, now evoked paroxysms of inexpressible hatred, of desire only to debase further the unwilling victim of my orgiastic passions. If only now I could compel his discomfort with a flood of the result of pleasure, of consummation, such as a man who defiles a woman's mouth can do! My own pleasurable exudations were the merest drippings. How I wanted to torture and degrade him!

I still held him to me, my hands pulling wildly at his hair. And now—oh, how can I confess such depravity, reader, how can I explain it—except by the insidious savagery of Russia that was tearing from me another layer of civilization's veneer? Now, with mad, diabolical malice, I called upon another internal reservoir . . . my bladder . . . with a supreme effort of will . . . I could feel the thin warm stream force its way slowly through the enspasmed channels of my urethra—till at last it gained release—and as I viciously held his tortured mouth to my cunt, I poured into him the liquid of a different form of relief—till it overflowed his lips. . .

I let him fall away to the floor, where he lay looking up at me with insane adoration; but with a mad, perverted passion, I sprang up, and with widespread thighs continued to pour down upon his face and chest so long as I could the warm slow-trickling stream. He made no effort to avoid the cruel deluge. When the last drop was fitfully squeezed from the distended soaking lips of my cunt, I fell back on the chair exhausted—relieved, but overcome with remorse. If my victim had been a man of real caliber, he would have thrown me down, raped my mouth and subjected me to like treatment. I deserved it, I might even have enjoyed it, what with all the salacious perverted possibilities I was momentarily unearthing in my soul. But he continued lying on the floor, passively. As I leaned back, still panting softly, my eyes shut, I reached out with my foot and felt his wet body. He quivered at the contact, and took my foot to kiss it.

"Circe! Divine enchantress!" he murmured. "Look how you make swine of men!" I wrenched myself free. I was so surfeited, so disgusted with him.

I had the greatest difficulty driving him away—for of course, I could not have endured him for the rest of the night. He loved me more devotedly than ever, he told me; he would sleep at my door. I threatened to call the police. He went at last. When I had bathed and returned to my boudoir, I found that, whether intentionally or by oversight, he had left his knout behind. I have treasured it since as a memento of a madness that I might all to easily forget and repudiate.

# CHAPTER SIX

Some days later, despite the admonition of Count B., my protector, I mastered the courage to call upon the monk Rasputin at his office on the Nevski Prospect. Here was a man who would doubtless make history, of whom so many strange tales were told that I could not resist the desire to meet him and see for myself.

When I seated myself in his waiting room, there were at least twenty other people ahead of me; but when the monk emerged from his inner holy of holies, he picked me out immediately as the most attractive woman present —of course, women came first—and led me within. Seating me on the edge of a leather-covered sofa, Grigori Efimovich Rasputin drew up a chair and sat opposite facing me. Boldly as he, I returned his close scrutiny. His great head was covered with ill-kempt brown hair, parted in the middle and hanging in damp strands over his forehead and neck. His whole face was overgrown by a heavy brown beard, the extreme lowest extremity of which he would nip between the thumb and forefinger of his veined right hand as if to accentuate its length. His skin was pockmarked and scarred. All in all, he seemed quite as unattractive and disappointing a sight as any other Russian muzhik might present. But his eyes were nonetheless fascinating and irresistable. They were pale blue and watery, yet beneath their crouching bushy brows they possessed a compelling power that seemed to pierce and penetrate to one's depths.

As we sat, he pressed my knees between

his—an affront which I overlooked for the time. A lewd sensual grin hovered about his lips.

"What brings you here, my daughter?" he spoke sanctimoniously. "I can see that you come from afar."

"I have come for your blessing, Father," I lied.

"Have you been to communion yet, my daughter?"

"No, Father."

"It is first necessary, my daughter, that you have part of Christ's divine body within you. It is only then, when you feel His holy flesh mingling with yours, that you can experience the efficacy of prayer." He leered suggestively and took one of my hands within his, tickling my palm with his thick, coarse fingers. "But since you have traveled so far for my blessing, I will not send you away empty. I am the vicar of Christ. His essence flows in my veins. I can grant you communion such as will make you feel His divine presence within you, more certainly, more ecstatically than if you had swallowed all the sacred wafers in Christendom." He pressed my knees more closely and put his hand on my bosom. I moved away. He went on speaking as if he had not noticed my rebuff.

"I can see, little daughter, that you are tormented by the desire to sin—else you would not have come here." He laughed vulgarly.

"Well, why not? So long as you repent. And what could find more favor in the eyes of the Lord than that you should sin with a holy man, and thus sinning, rid him as well as yourself of burdening lusts? What do you say, my daughter? You will thank me and bless me when it is over."

I was frightened. The massive proportions, the general hideousness of the man, all revolted me. And his strange, compelling manner aroused all my most innate oppositions.

"No, Father," I said nervously, "I understand. But I have no desire to sin, really. I will go to communion tomorrow—that is, the ordinary communion—and return for your blessing some other day." I arose to go. He laid his heavy hands on my shoulders and pressed me back to my seat. His peculiar eyes turned from light to darkest blue, glittering with sensual desire.

"It is the will of God!" he rasped, "and I must enforce it! Would you dare to match your foolish youth against my matured wisdom?" Then his voice became soft and insinuating again. He spoke in a low passionate whisper now, murmuring strange voluptuous words that seemed to weaken all my body and enleaden my limbs. I felt his hot breath upon me. His devouring eyes roved over my body. His hands followed.

"What opulent curves! Yes, I will administer the holy sacrament! I will fuck you!" He employed the ugly word for it, "yebotch." I was on the verge of yielding, but with a supreme effort of will I shook him off.

"No! no!" I cried. "Let me go! I hate you!"

He threw me back upon the couch and leaned over me, transfixing me with his burning eyes. All my powers of resistance ebbed away.

"Now, now," he murmured with a strange,

soothing monotony, "everything will be all right. You do not hate me, my daughter—and you will love me afterwards. If you refuse me, you will regret it all your days. You will dream of me nights, and long for me. But see, you no longer resist me. I do not force you, you want me. You want this—" And laughing lewdly once more, he whipped out his brutal muzhik truncheon. I shuddered. All my intellect and senses revolted against my being the victim of this demon; but my body was paralyzed, pinned down by the man's hypnotic powers.

Now I could see only his gleaming, mysterious eyes, with their crafty, lustful expression. I could feel his hands raising my dress to my waist, I could feel him pulling my silk step-ins down toward my knees. I wanted to scream. I couldn't. I wanted to resist, to spring up and escape. I could make no move. If only I could wrench my gaze away from his—but I could not so much as close my eyelids or turn away my head.

His huge bar of flesh lay on my cold ivory thighs, groping its way blindly upward toward their culmination. In a moment he would be rending my tenderest tissues . . .

Just then the telephone bell rang. He paused for a moment, but went on with his rape, unwilling to abandon his advantage. The phone rang more insistently. Angrily he cursed in Russian; but the noisy distraction continued. He rose from my cataleptic form and went to the telephone. In that moment his spell was broken. I recovered control of my limbs and sprang quickly to my feet to make for the door. But it took me some time to readjust my clothes and a moment later he was by my side.

"Never mind, little daughter," he said, laughing good-naturedly, "that was Tzarskoje Tselo—the imperial palace—calling me. Even as you were resisting me, the Princess Olga phones to beg me to join her for some of the divine administration that you so foolishly refuse. So I might as well save it for her. Yes, I have fucked not only the beautiful Princess Olga, but also her sisters Maria and Tatyana, and Anastasia. The Tzarina herself has never refused me—and know you that the impotent Nikolai himself is pleased to have me do it for him. Ha, ha, little foreigner, if you remain in Petrograd long enough, you will soon learn that this—" and he brandished proudly his still stiff and rampant limb—"is the divine sceptre that rules all of Holy Russia!"

He replaced the sacred root in his trousers and led me politely to the door.

"Show mademoiselle to a droshky!" he directed his plump, fuckable maid, Dunia. Unbeknownst to me at the time, he had one of many secret agents follow me to my hotel to learn my address.

The very next afternoon, as I sat alone in my boudoir reading with some slight difficulty a Russian edition of the secret memoirs of Catherine the Great, inflaming myself with the pictures of mad Tartar lasciviousness, the door opened and in walked Rasputin, unannounced.

Whether of my own volition, or because of some inexplicable posthypnotic influence that he had cast over me, I had been thinking of him all night and all day. What exactly could be the nature of this power over women that he was accredited with? What was this fascination that he held for queens and princesses? Something told me that I must yield to him and discover for myself. Something within me had impelled me to wish for him—and here he was.

I received him calmly, picking up one of my dainty garters that were strewn about and laying it between the pages of my book to keep my place. He was quite friendly and apologetic.

"Do you still think of me so harshly as you did yesterday?" he asked. It was useless to contest his purpose. I knew his power, the futility of further resistance. I might as well save the situation by making the best of it.

"No, Father," I answered coyly, "you were right. I have regretted my foolish refusal."

"Ah, that is much better," he said, and proceeding immediately to remove his caftan and boots, he sat down beside me and opened my negligee a trifle to appraise the texture and solidity of my breasts. When his will was not crossed, it was obvious that Grigori could be a most charming gentleman. For my reassurance, he began to outline his religious beliefs of sin and repentance. I yawned.

"Oh, that's all right, Father. We're both in the same business of relieving people of their sinful lusts—only I'm a bit more direct in my manner of doing it."

He understood and laughed heartily at the joke.

"Then there is no need of prefacing my practice with preaching," he said good-naturedly, and removing my negligee from me

116

he pushed my naked form back on the couch and hastily stripped off his own remaining clothes. His body was spare, but massively and muscularly built. His organ—despite, or perhaps because of, its no doubt frequent usage, was colossal, frightening, and was surrounded by a profusion of crisp black hair. His huge love-purse resembled a pair of young coconuts, and promised an unprecedented quantity of love's elixir.

As he lowered himself upon me, his thickly begrown hairy chest tickled the erect upstanding nipples of my tenderer charms. A moment later his fearful equipment imprinted itself on my belly, then, sliding it lower down over my silky mount, he brought the monstrous blood-gorged head to bear upon my quaking crimson tidbit. Tried as my parts were by many encounters with other not insignificant Moscovite weapons, my sensitive little recess seemed but a sorry match for his unwieldy bludgeon.

Against the delicate mossy gates his assaulting engine pressed firmly; but scarcely more than half the diameter of his giant cylinder could my nether mouth encompass, even with the best of its intentions. With my own fingers, which hastened to the specific scene of the affray, I stretched wide first one side of the moist excited folds and then the other; but even at this he was in only lip deep. Firmly he continued pressing inward. Anxious as my cunny was to receive him, the disproportion was so great that I blanched and winced with the pain of the distention. He noted my suffering.

"Now, little daughter," the monk uttered in a soothing tone, "I can see that you are not accustomed to the virile members of holy Russia. But forget that part of you that aches. Look into my eyes. See—there is now no more pain for you. All hurt is gone. You can experience only pleasure henceforth."

And surely enough, as if an anesthetic had been introduced into my throbbing parts, the pain vanished, and now, though the membranes of my sheath were partially numbed by his beneficent hypnotism, I could sense his monstrous wedge sliding slowly into the grateful scabbard until it was entirely within my body, clasped tightly in the hot moist flesh.

"Now you can feel me once more," he said. "Your womb clutches the head of my member. You are ready to enjoy."

I was. With the lifting of the spell, my organ awoke to a delicious state of pleasurable sensitivity, all its glands opening to add lubrication for the delightful movements to come.

"Fuck me now, Father!" I moaned, beginning to writhe impatiently under the impalement of his soul-satisfying shaft. He did . . . and oh, as that solid stuffing of velvety flesh moved in and out of my hot voluptuous channel, I bounded frantically up to meet him with a violence that would have at once unseated any less expert rider than he.

With such divine treatment, it could not take long for me to reach the acme of bliss —which I did, with a long low wail of rapture, my hips continuing to pump madly up and down to bring forth the easing balm of his discharge. But staunch and self-controlled, he held on within me, requiring even further fires to melt the rampant rivet that sustained the incomparable tight conjuction of our heav-

118

ing bodies. For all my efforts to bring him on, I merely worked myself into a second frenzy. Now I lost all voluntary ability for co-ordinated movement; but the exudations of my first orgasm had oiled his stiff stake so superbly that he was able, despite my wild fitful motions, to fuck back and forth with fierce, full, quick strokes. A few dispatching thrusts from his strong loins sent me again to the heights of ecstasy, and my womb poured forth a second oblation to the god of love.

But still his huge joy-giving assailant continued fully potent within my enspasmed cunt, uncompromisingly withholding its own creamy offering of surrender. A triumphant smile adorned Grigori's face when I opened my fevered eyes to look at him. I begged him to finish off quickly and let me rest from the already excessive pleasure he had bestowed upon me.

"No no, my daughter!" he said hoarsely, still pounding fiercely away, "I must completely drain you of your sin!"

My oversensitive membranes protested; the muscles of my cunt closed with steely desperation about his bar to restrain his maddening frictions; but it was useless. His strong engine rode down all the delicate resistance that the wet warm folds could offer, and soon another climax was spurting its fitful fires through my veins and nerves, leaving my whole body stiff and rigid with wild lustful pleasure, choking my screams of ecstasy in my very throat.

And *still* he fucked me! Vigorously, unceasingly. The combination that Nature has set over the treasure-source of woman's pleasure, the exact number of turns and twists and pushes and frictions that ordinarily are required to induce the nervous system to open its joy-valves and pour out the amount of voluptuousness that it determines the woman can endure—all these judicious restraints were suspended, and my womb, my glands, never before so continuously and violently called-upon, yielded up the keys as it were, opened wide their ducts, and poured out their ecstatic emulsions in an almost ceaseless spasm of spending.

For over an hour and a half he kept up the divine—I could as well say diabolical—workings of his august, tireless tool. Long before this time I was completely overcome with pleasure, more dead than alive—unconscious except for the sense of his continual plunging in and out of me, my involuntarily responsive thrusts, and ever and again the stinging flare of sensation that tokened another orgasm. I must have come no less than twelve distinct times, not counting the numerous partial thrills that I was too far gone to keep track of and the final frenzy of sensual titillation that kept me helplessly hysterical in the last half hour of his erect yard's relentless application.

For a time, as I have said, I fainted entirely away into a state of flaming lubricity that was now soothing and now torturing. When I came to, yet another tremendous orgasm was climbing to my brain. My congested cunt was brimming over with joys still exclusively its own, the whole tender passage still plugged up by the volume of his immense limb.

"Mother of God!" Rasputin roared suddenly,

"I am coming! Sacred Virgin, receive my offering!" Grasping my buttocks to draw my wildly heaving body closer, he pushed and drove and tore within my over-stimulated membranes more fiercely than ever. His face was livid with lust. His breath whistled sharply between his teeth and down his beard. My own breathing had long since ceased except for some spasmodic gasps now and then.

Suddenly his whole body stiffened. His bursting member swelled perceptibly within me—and just as I came—with one final crushing thrust he poured into my irritated vitals a hot flood—or rather a long series of spurting jets, like a quick fusillade of shots—of his copious, thick, manly virus, that soothed the burning convolutions of my cunt and left me squirming and wriggling and screaming with the divine relief.

For whole minutes it seemed he continued ejaculating his warm glutinous cream into me. My parts overflowed, my thighs and anus were inundated as never before or since.

At last he withdrew his huge lolling member —which, even as seen through my joy-clouded eyes, made me shudder with the reminiscence of tingling sensations. I was still moaning and panting and beating my arms and legs about like a person possessed—for the hypersensitivity of my body, indescribable, ticklish, convulsing at the least touch, did not pass easily.

The monk, himself entirely recovered, made me drink some strong vodka from a flask— and gradually I revived. Now I knew the secret of his fame. His was an accomplishment that any man might be proud of; the ability not only to satisfy the most ardent of women, but to give her more than she has ever dared to dream was possible.

Seated beside me now, Grigori chatted on in a pleasant manner, helping himself frequently to the contents of his flask and becoming more and more confiding and boastful.

"You don't believe that this has pushed the Empress of Russia, do you? Well, she has even kissed it. And I know her so well that I could tell you the exact number of wrinkles in her cunt. When first I met her, she had fitted up a private subterranean chapel outside the palace, especially for me, where none were allowed to intrude. Here, while the Tzar thought his dear spouse was at prayer, we would fuck for hours. I—Grigori Efimovich Rasputin, simple abused little muzhik of Povroskoe—fucking the Empress of Russia!

"But Olga, the eldest daughter—ah, she's a sweet piece! And Princess Maria, too. And the Tzaritza's younger sister—you know, the beautiful nun. I've driven the devil out of all of them. And all the attractive ladies in and out of court. Why their husbands consider it an honor to have me hallow their wives' cunts with this!"

Such bragging soon put the temporarily wilted subject of his discussion in a boasting mood again. Feeling sinful once more, the monk began making application for additional salvation. But I was still so sensitive in the requisite sanctuary that I had to induce him to consent to the French substitute that I proffered.

So I set to; but I could scarcely get even the head of his bar into my mouth, try as I might, and I had to confine myself for the most part to external stimulations. Seated on a cushion on the floor between his knees, I did my best, rolling my tongue over the huge ruby knob, stroking the delicate grove of the underside, inserting the tip of my tongue into the scarlet, sensitive urethra, and sucking on it when I could. Rasputin watched with voluptuous interest while I attended earnestly to business. The gigantic proportion of my task, the honor of sucking this master-prober that had plumbed all the choicest and most aristocratic cunts of Russia, all made me strive to make this the finest lingual fuck I had ever administered. It was.

"Ah, God! What have I been missing! I must teach the Princess!" he murmured as my agile tongue made spirals about the swollen flesh of his capital and my soft practiced hands stroked the long shaft of his pulsating feeler.

It took a long time, perhaps all of fifteen minutes, for this delicious titillation to bring him on; but at last I could judge from his heavy breathing as well as by other unmistakable symptoms that the supreme moment approached. I knew what to expect from his capacious oversized reservoirs, and just as he stiffened in the final throes of pleasurable ejaculation. I placed my fingers firmly about his spouting member, allowed only as much to spring past my lips as my mouth could at one time hold, clamping off the rest by pressure upon the delicate canal. The intensity of his prolonged and intercepted pleasure caused him to roar with agonized delight. When I released the pressure on his bursting pego the damned-up torrent of thick hot sperm shot out with inconceivable force, flooding my mouth again and overflowing to my breasts and abdomen.

"Bless you, bless you, my daughter!" he exclaimed, overwhelmed. "I am just beginning to appreciate the French!"

"And I have only this afternoon learned to appreciate Russia," I returned in kind, swallowing the last benefits of the melee.

When the holy monk at last was about to leave, he in gratefulness wished me to take a heap of currency that he drew carelessly from his pockets. I refused. In its stead, he forced me to accept a beautiful signet ring, bearing the imperial Russian double eagle, that he had received from the Tzaritza. I cherish it still.

# CHAPTER SEVEN

A few more weeks gave me my fill of the Russian capital, and I transferred to Moscow for a few days with the count and some friends. But soon I tired even of this more lively metropolis—though I couldn't decide whether to return to Paris or to do some further globe-trotting.

To put an end to my quandary, a strange proposal came that fired my imagination and set my footsteps southward to encounter the most dangerous adventure of my life.

Ivan Rudschenko it was, a wealthy land speculator from Rostovnadanu who told me first of a Baron Grigor Feodorov, who in this modern day and age carried on a huge plantation in the South of Russia (the Zaparuzhti) with slaves, a harem, and all the insignia of medieval autocracy. A harem could mean only one thing to me: fucking—and lots of it—perhaps some strong spicy competition. I became interested. Ivan confessed that the baron was a friend and neighbor of his, and that oftimes he had been commissioned to recruit additional wives or concubines for him. He was returning home soon. If I was interested in joining him, I would be well paid for my time—10,000 rubles in advance. Somehow, I was developing great confidence in my ability to get along, or to handle even the strangest of men. And my curiosity and adventurousness tempted me further. After all, I thought, what has a woman to lose after her maidenhead, especially when she is willing to be fucked, sucked and even buggered? I little dreamt what lay in store for me.

I accompanied him. Two days of travel on southward almost to the shores of the Black Sea, and then off into the Caucasus by some branch line to Ekaterinodar. Even here our journey did not end. I had to endure seven hours of traveling in a springless wagon over miles of miserable roads that led eastward into the mountains.

Whether during all this time my relations with Ivan were platonic or no, I leave it to the astuteness of the reader to judge. As our intimacy deepened, he seemed to show more and more regret for my undertaking. He even intimated that I could still return to Moscow without forfeiting his deposit. Since it was not the money which had lured me hither, I refused to abandon the enterprise; but by the time we reached the end of our journey, some of his ill-concealed uneasiness had communicated itself to me, and I was especially disquieted by the somberness of the ancient godforsaken castle that finally turned out to be our destination.

I was led into a great medieval hall, and here I made the acquaintance of the baron. Typically enough, in my first glimpse of him, he wore heavy iron-shod boots and a high shaggy fur hat, and with whip in hand was engaged in instigating two huge ferocious wolfhounds to do bloody battle upon each other.

He paused in his occupation and greeted me with a sort of sneering supercilious politeness that, in externalities at least, proclaimed him fairly civilized. He even addressed some words in French to me when he learned my supposed nationality. As he spoke, his deep bass voice, his dark menacing eyes and ugly beard, all struck me with a conviction that I had met him somewhere before. Yet reason told me that such was impossible. Unless in another incarnation, I had never been to Russia before—and certainly my own span of life thus far hadn't been so extensive as to make it likely that I had met him elsewhere and forgotten. Nor could I think of any other person of my acquaintance that I might be confusing him with. This strong sense of recognition was doubtless the phenomenon of *deja vu* that psychologists write of: the mere fantasy of a tired mind; but yet, for the life of me, I could not cease racking my brain to place him—and the more I worried, the further from a satisfactory solution I seemed to get.

I was shown into the library. Here I was left alone while the baron and Ivan retired to settle some business between themselves. To occupy the time I glanced curiously over the many cases of books. There were hundreds of volumes on flagellation. There were numerous volumes devoted to the cruelties of the Roman Caesars and of the Christian Inquisitors, and any number of histories of the bloody perverted exploits of the Marshal Gilles de Rais, the Bluebeard of the Middle Ages.

My host's other interests it appeared were even less reassuring. Over the fireplace hung a horribly realistic portrayal of *The Slaughter of The Innocents*. In the corner stood a huge couch equipped with steel manacles. On the desk, lying on an open volume of de Sade's bloody book *Justine,* was an odd diabolical little thumbscrew affair that was obviously an instrument of torture. My anxiety quickly

127

grew to horror. I must rejoin Ivan and get away from here. All panicky, I rushed out of the door into the hall—full into the arms of Baron Feodorov. He held me firmly.

"What is the matter?" he demanded sternly. As he spoke, his dark shaggy eyebrows twitched nervously up and down like fluttering bat-wings.

"Ivan . . . I want Ivan!" I gasped.

"Too late," he told me, "Ivan has gone. What did you want him for?"

"Nothing . . . only . . . only I don't like this place. I don't wish to stay here."

"Indeed, my choice little French demoiselle! But you are all bought and paid for. You *must* stay." He leered horribly and reached insolently for my bosom.

"Let me go!" I exclaimed, "or I'll scream!"

He was convulsed with gargantuan laughter.

"Scream!" He pinched my arm viciously. "By all means scream! A woman's screams are music to my ears. But if you think to scream for anything other than my pleasure, you are unfortunately wrong. Even if this building were not soundproof, which it is, everyone within a radius of fifty versts belongs to me, and far from daring to come to your aid, they would return you to me in short order if you tried to escape. Moreover, the entrance to this castle is never unguarded. Now, scream again!"

I forgot my horror in the fascination of my growing conviction of familiarity. His very words, I seemed to have heard before—even the cruel grip of his hands was an experience that seemed linked with him in some vague irreducible past.

He dragged me back into the library and threw me upon the couch.

"Woman!" he pronounced ominously, "I am going to strip your clothes from your body, chain you down to this torture rack, and rape you! Now, what do you think of that?"

I decided to make the best of it.

"Nothing," I replied, as serenely as I could, "except that you needn't trouble either to remove my clothes forcibly or to strap me down. I know what I'm here for—and I like it. If I didn't, I wouldn't be here. So why talk of rape? You can't take away from me anything that I'm just as anxious to give as you are to receive. Shall I undress?"

This speech, though it cost me some effort, I was certain would mollify him. But no. As if infinitely aggravated by my suggestion of complicity, he turned red with anger, the veins of his forehead and neck stood out like whipcords, and without another word, he dealt me a blow in the face that brought involuntary tears welling to my eyes.

The sight of my pain enlivened him. His hands felt all my parts brutally, then suddenly, with impatience, he tore my gown from me with a single ripping movement. Where had I seen that bearded, diabolically leering face before? Where in my lifetime had this very same scene been before enacted? Another tearing sound and my silk slip lay in shreds at my feet. I stood before him now clad only in short silk panties and a narrow satin brassiere from which the flesh of my breasts overflowed alluringly. To forestall him, I reached behind me to open the confining band. He tore my hand away and ripped it off forcibly. My most delicate ivory contours, freed in this profane manner, he squeezed and molded till I was sick with pain. But even this, it seemed, had happened to me before. A tearing jerk at my dainty step-ins, and through the blur of my tears I looked down on the complete nudity of my body, white, except where relieved by the dark delta that marked the conjunction of my thighs and by my black silk hose—which could scarcely be considered articles of clothing or protection since they seem invariably to act as provocatives to men.

Throwing me back upon the couch, he locked my ankles and wrists with the manacles that I had before noted, holding all my limbs widespread perforce, and keeping me in every way completely subject to his whim. For a moment he talked about my intimate charms with words of cynical admiration, working himself into a frenzy of lust and anger. Nor could he forego the villainous pleasure of threatening me with his slender vicious knife that he drew from his belt.

"Look upon this!" he roared. "As soon as I grow tired of your vile cunt, I will slice you to ribbons, piece by piece!"

His tone—his words! Where, *where*, had I heard them? His attitude . . . the strange sense of familiarity that troubled me overshadowed even the fears I might have felt at his deadly threats. I had lived through just such an experience before—so why be frightened by it?

He drew out his member. It was huge and fierce, vein-knotted and blunt-headed. He fell upon me, brought the truncheon approximately to the breach, and without troubling to entrench or open the way, lunged brutally inward. If he had exercised the conventional firm gentleness of any other lover, if he had properly stimulated in me the necessary secretions to lubricate my vulva, I would even then have experienced trouble coping with his monstrous engine. But as it was, the rending pain, the agony of his single-plunged onslaught on my unprepared membranes, was so sharp, so unbearable, that I screamed out and nearly fainted away.

Never before had I experienced such horrible suffering. It must be just an awful nightmare, I told myself. Never before? *Nightmare?* In the short moment that he crashed into my body's tenderest parts, in the moment of my most excrutiating agony, the strange sense of a scene relived reached its most unendurable, insanity-courting intensity. "Put the great — in the — *and turned it!*"

The baron, obtaining complete insertion of his cruel probe, had ground it about within the lacerated folds of my cunny. With infinitely redoubled pain, it flashed upon my tortured consciousness:—Front de Boeuf, the great key, that horrible dream of years before! Only *this* was reality: the nightmare seeking its fulfillment in waking life. And this overwhelming sensation of yielding to an annihilating torture, that too was in the dream. Only from this reality there could be no escape, no awakening.

I struggled against the impulse to faint, desperately clinging to consciousness, refusing the insidious invitation to oblivion and death. I would laugh at the pain! And surely enough, echoing my thought, I heard, as from a great distance, a hysterical female laugh that I recognized as my own.

I continued laughing, though my teeth were clenched. By associating, by one of those phenomena that this is scarcely the place to explain, my determination and my laughter brought me fresh vitality and resistance. My mind cleared, my emotions subsided. Pleasure or pain, what was the difference? Both were violent experiences, which, like tangents in trigonometry carried to infinity, become equivalent, though antipodically opposite in their origins. I rallied in every way, confirming by an effort of will as it were, all my racking pains to the localities from which they emanated.

My assailant continued plunging back and forth within me. There was now no question of pleasure for me. Indeed, as he raised his body and withdrew his engine between strokes, I could see it covered with a rich crimson that was my blood. Whether naturally or perversely, despite the passionate fury which ordinarily hastens a man's ebullition in direct proportion to its heat, the baron showed no signs of coming. To shorten the agonizing alliance of our bodies, to at least deprive his weapon of a share of its cruel excessive stiffness by bringing on the unstarching, I had recourse to one of woman's most ancient devices—that to date I had had but little necessity for simulating. Within the limitations of my manacles I set about to employ all possible subtleties of cooperative movement—counterfeiting, so far as I was able, the symptoms of approaching pleasure myself.

Instantly, he stopped me with a blow, withdrawing his encarnadined weapon.

"I *take* my pleasure!" he growled. "I do not share it. Your enjoyment, whether real or pretended, subtracts from mine and distracts me. Later I will cut away your clitoris to ensure that it is I who use you, and not you me! And meanwhile. . ."

He adjusted the chains that held me so that my legs and thighs were high in the air. In this way both my front and rear were equally visible and accessible to him. Without turning me over, without troubling to employ any easing lubricant, he brought his part against the lower and more tightly puckered gateway to my body, and rammed it fiercely inward . . .

How fortunate that someone more gentle than he had already opened that path; how thankful I was for the moistness on his monstrous tool, even of my cunt's blood—else, surely, I would have been burst asunder. Even as it was, he hurt me cruelly. But happily, in this tight unnatural sheath of mine, it did not take him long to consummate. As his crisis approached, however, the bloodthirsty baron sank his teeth sharply into my bare shoulder—a moment later flooding my bowels with the thick spurts of his fiery essence.

His fierce growl faded into a low moan as the pleasure melted his over-tensed body. When he withdrew from my dripping anus, he was a changed man—a bit cold perhaps, but rational and dignified—chastened, if anything, by his cruel orgiastic outburst. With the deft hands of a surgeon he dressed my bleeding shoulder.

"Till next time," he said. "I do not require

that you should suffer at such times as I am not with you. In the intervals between my pleasures, my women are well treated—fattened up, if you will, for the tortures I subject them to. Ultimately, of course, you all go to the bone-heap."

I took this opportunity to ask him whether he really meant to execute his murderous threats.

"Why not," he laughed, "if it suits my pleasures?"

"But have you no fear of being held accountable by the law, if not by God?"

"God," he laughed again, "is a delusion of the weak, a fantasy for slaves who hope to get in the hereafter the kind of justice which their low minds conceive and which this world will not afford them. And as for the law—the law is of the strong—and in this part of Russia, I am the law."

"But I have friends—influential friends—" I told him, "in Moscow, in Petrograd—and of course in Paris. You cannot keep me here long before there will be an investigation. Count . . ."

He interrupted.

"Does anyone beside Ivan know you came here?" he asked, seemingly perturbed.

"Yes!" I lied, "I was about to tell you. Count B. and Baron R. They tried to dissuade me. They asked me not to remain away long."

He was silent. But I knew my ruse had succeeded. My captor now, it was obvious, would think twice before inflicting any serious injury upon me.

# CHAPTER EIGHT

I was taken away to the women's apartments. I shall not record the details of all that followed. Nor shall I give the accounts of the eight various women who were for two long horrible months my companions in misery. Suffice it that their tales of our master's bloody practices were replete with horror—and worthy of comparison with the worst in the Marquis de Sade's writings—so much so, indeed, and so similar to them, that I shall omit all but the very latter part of this nightmare, referring the reader to the annals of psychopathology for fuller descriptions of what such monsters are capable of.

One of the number of prisoners, a beautiful young girl of sixteen, I was horrified to learn, was the legitimate daughter of our captor by one of his earlier wives, now long since deceased as a result of his criminal mistreatment and this delicate flower of maidenhood the incestuous villain showed especial preference for in his cruel sadistic orgies. In one of his more rational moments, I ventured to question him. Without morals as I was myself, I could not comprehend any justification for his thus torturing what was in effect his own flesh and blood.

"On the contrary, mademoiselle," he told me with a supercilious smile, "the fact that she is my own flesh and blood, as you put it so quaintly, the fact that she is forbidden to me by all the laws of man and church, makes the use of her body all the more interesting and pleasurable. And since she is so closely a part of me, since she is in truth beholden to me for bestowing life upon her, who should more justly be entitled to the benefits of her body than I, her father, her creator? A king, by waging war, has the unquestioned right to the lives of all his subjects, has he not? What lessor right, pray, should a father have? The old Spartan law, giving to parents the privilege of life or death over their children was a sound one. And my only regret is that I have not fucked more daughters into existence so that I might have more of them to abuse when my little Sonya is maimed beyond use by my various voluptuous experiments. If I haven't permitted myself more offspring heretofore, it is because to bear children constitutes for women such a deep gratification as to overweigh the sum total of all cruelties inflicted in their begetting—and that I cannot countenance. But you are an intelligent woman, mademoiselle. No doubt you practice contraception—whereby you deprive the male seed of its life. Perhaps too you have induced abortion in yourself, thus murdering a living foetus. Where do you draw the line? No doubt you are ready with the usual justifications. You will indicate the general overabundance and wastefulness of nature. If you are humanitarian, you may point out the overpopulation of this small planet of ours whereby plagues, famines and wars are brought about. Exactly so. Nature *is* wasteful. Of the monthly ovum that woman's body ripens, only one in twelve at most can be impregnated. Of the millions of spermatozoa that stream from a man in the single divine execution of God's own indicated method of coitus, only one at best can reach its goal.

What then if I choose to consider this particular bit of engendered seed that becomes my offspring with the same carelessness as Nature, or with the same indifference as I regard that which it pleases me to lose so profusely in my frequent pleasures?"

"But how can you compare a living, sentient being to a drop of sperm?" I exclaimed, horrified at his cold sophistry.

"Ah, now you are getting sentimental, my dear Madeleine," he went on, "and being so, your objections show an astonishing lack of insight that is unspeakably deplorable in a person of your apparent intelligence. First of all, none but our own feelings possess reality —and to attempt to base a system of ethics on any other presumption is not only erroneous, but altogether impossible. Do but consider. Can you justly attribute your own and my exquisite refinements of taste to the average witless Russian serf? Do you not know that the common herd exists only to serve us and to be beaten? But more pertinently, do we stop to consider the feelings of the beast or fowl that we slaughter for our food, or vivisect out of scientific curiousity? We do not. We may become vegetarian; but how can we say that the onion, torn away from its living roots, experiences less anguish than the steer whose throat is cut—or that the stupid muzhik whom I may hang for my amusement suffers more? Indisputably, all life is sustained by preying upon weaker species, and we must shut our ears to the cries of our victims, or better still, learn to enjoy them as testimony to our own strength. Forget the sickly maxims of Christ. They are all very

137

well for the hopelessly weak. Naturally enough, the lamb cannot understand why the wolf should want to devour it. But interrogate the wolf and you will find his viewpoint as creditable as the other's, more so, since he has the power to put it into execution.

"Now, human beings, despite the fact that they are members of the same species, and for all the drivel of republican ideas, are unequally endowed by nature and by circumstance. Should the strong then forego their strength to accommodate and perpetuate the weak when the necessary trend in life is the survival of the fittest? Most certainly not.

"And now we come to the question of the relations of the sexes. That they are of unequal strength, mentally and economically as well as physically, goes without saying. That there is a basic antagonism between the sexes, and that whatever in their relations benefits the one must always be at the expense of the other, must be conceded also after a moment's consideration. Women are by nature, or perhaps from necessity, perfidious and contemptible, with that detestable pettiness of conduct that may indeed be the sole defense of the weak, but cannot be construed as an admirable quality from any viewpoint. Give them the least freedom and they will betray you, fastening upon you the fruit of another man's seed, bringing back to your bed the diseases of the first fool that flatters them with a bit of chivalry—that hypocritical invention of petty adulterers, who, for their stolen amours, can well afford to disregard the codes of domestic discipline. The only remaining alternative is that of the Middle Ages—

chastity belts, unrelaxed intimidation by all the devices of spirit-crushing cruelty.

"Only if society could exist without women would there be any such thing as real happiness or true nobility of body, mind and soul. So it was that the Spartans, those paragons of all the social virtues, in view of the great contempt in which they held their women, had to pass laws to compel men to propogate with them.

"Nevertheless, to those of us who have not been entirely emancipated from the filthy necessity for them, who from earliest childhood have had our sex urges misdirected and fixed upon the goal of the female when our own kind would have served much better—to us unfortunates, sex attraction must coexist alongside even the worst antagonism toward this opposite species. Is it surprising then that some of us should detest and torture this cloven sex that thus withholds from us independence and perfection, even as we acknowledge their necessity? Or, to put it more crudely, must we tenderly love and cherish the night-pot that is essential for our animal needs? Or is the robber to be thankful to the victim, whom he has robbed by sheer force and at his own risk? Obviously not.

"But to approach the problem from a more personal side: that of the necessary enjoyment of the carnal act. That it is requisite or even desirable for the woman to share with the man in the pleasure of their connection is a ridiculous fallacy held to only by the most preposterously egotistical of men, or by efeminates of my own sex, who, weak in their own capacity for enjoyment, must content themselves with flattering their vanity by contemplating the pleasures they imagine they are bestowing upon their female incumbent. In truth, however, they fail to note that to share a joy is to be robbed of most of it; that to savor it fully one must shut one's self in with one's faculties and concentrate exclusively on the intensification of one's own pleasure. To permit the distraction of concerning one's self with the satisfaction of a creature outside you, a dubious thing at best, is to fritter away the precious moments of one's own gratification. Concede then that it is only foolish pride that attaches such a condition to enjoyment, and that only one's own personal feelings possess reality."

"But Baron," I expostulated earnestly, "do you mean to assert that the state of one's partner means nothing then? That the reflection of reaction of the other's sensations does nothing toward increasing one's own pleasure?"

"Well, perhaps in the strength of my conviction I have overstated the case," the baron resumed, "but now we come to the real point of the entire matter. The voluptuousness of sex connection is a sort of frenzied vibration, produced not only by the degree of one's activity, but also by the stimulation of one's imagination, by the inflaming remembrance of all one's past thwarted desires or fancies, and finally, by the realization of the actual presence of the wanton female object. Now even granting you that the irritation of this object can sharpen one's own lubricity, and that the man is most flattered by seeing the object experiencing the greatest possible sensation, it by no means follows that it must be pleasure that he bestows. On the contrary, it is far more flattering to one's self or to one's sense of power to force a woman than to woo or bribe her by dividing your enjoyment with her. Benevolence is the weak tea of existence, good enough for women and weaklings; but tyranny alone is the fiery vodka of self-assertion that man craves and should not forego. How much more intense is his pleasure, how much more speedily and fiercely does he arrive at his climax—and after all, this is the sole purpose of his engagement in the act, all inanities of unselfishness aside—if he can compell the woman *not* to enjoy and draw all of her attention toward himself. Delicacy does not add to the pleasures of the senses: it is noxious to it—connoting restraint, as it does, when complete surrender to all the ferocity of a basic hunger is necessary. So long as the man permits the woman to occupy herself with her own gratification, he does not himself enjoy, or at best, enjoys merely intellectually, chimerically, in a manner far inferior to that of the senses. Like the dog in Aesop he foresakes the bone for the shadow and gives over real enjoyments for illusions.

"And what illusions indeed! The simulation of pleasure by women is a most common occurrence, and so, the sum result of the altruistic man's tenderness and sweating and striving to satisfy his partner is that neither in the end is at all fulfilled or gratified. He has curbed his naturally impetuous passions for another's sake, while she, impatient for him to put an end to his unpleasant probing—for how few women indeed possess even the fraction of a man's desire for active passion—conceals her disgust and with a few artificial sighs or moans or quivers that the most susceptible of man must often doubt, gives the cue of release to her silly lover who has himself made the gratification of a strictly selfish impulse dependent upon an entirely doubtful and irrelevant reaction in another. I trust I have convinced you of this at least: that from the man's viewpoint, if pleasure exists ever or at all in the female object, it is absolutely hypothetical, indeterminate and unprovable. I take it as axiomatic that since selfishness is the first law of nature, it must be especially so in fornication—that most powerful of nature's manifestations. The woman's happiness or unhappiness then, should be a matter of complete indifference to the man so long as he himself is satisfied. His sensual reactions are entirely contained within his own organism—there is no kind of connection or relation between this object and himself except insofar as it is a mere means to a personal end. It would be madness then to occupy himself with the sensations of this external object at the expense of his own, or to renounce the improvement of his own pleasures to avoid causing her disappointment or pain.

"Perhaps I have disgressed somewhat; but by every road we reach the same conclusions. The feelings of another do not exist; but even if in our egoistic pride, we require some visible state of sensational turmoil in the woman in order to lash up the fury of our own consummation, that of pleasure in her is both weak and unreliable. Pain, however, is quantitatively the greatest of all possible sensations—as witness the fact that pain alone can burst the bounds of human endurance and cause extinction. To the onlooker too, there is no sensation more effectively stimulating than that of suffering. Its evidences are visible and certain, and, especially if we ourselves inflict it, cannot deceive us as those of pleasure, which, as I have said before, generally simulated by all women, are hardly ever felt by any. When we strike someone or are ourselves brought in forcible contact with some foreign object, we may be assured of the resulting sensation as perhaps the only certain cause and effect relation in this whole uncertain existence of ours. To strike a blow, too, is a natural form of self-expression, particularly and indisputably a part of the primitive rapine character of our sexual instinct. To give pleasure on the other hand, any number of difficult or even impossible conditions must exist. The woman must have the fundamental orgasmic capacity, which, incidentally, is not possessed at all by the greater number of your preposterous sex. She must be, to a nicety, in just the proper mood; must be delicately approached in just such and such a manner. And besides all this, what a great deal of health, strength and self-adoration is necessary on the part of the man to persist in producing this doubtful impression, which after all his efforts, he will generally fail to do. To bring about the feeling and manifestation of pain, however, requires nothing. The older, the uglier, the less capable of inspiring love a man is, the better he will succeed.

"To conclude my lengthy harangue, it is obvious that cruelty in the sex act is the natural procedure for those of us who are unhandsome or unamiable and consequently can never be sure that we are loved—for those of us defectives who from bitter experence have learned to be thoroughly certain of but one unpleasing truth: that it is impossible for anyone else to partake of what we feel, or even comprehend it. We forsake the vain pursuit of illusions, and live therefore in the continual affirmation of our selfishness."

The baron's voice trailed off into silence, leaving in its wake a deep rumbling sigh. I had listened to his speech spellbound, though confused by the unheard-of savagery of his philosophy. But now it all became vividly clear to me. His hate-seared countenance now bore an expression that was actually human. I almost thought too that I discerned a bit of moisture in those hard eyes that had probably never shed a tear. His closing words had furnished the key. Doubtless he had begun life like most of us, like myself, with a conviction of his own inferiority, with a timid humble craving for human understanding. Perhaps he had been disappointed in love. Perhaps the world had rebuffed him in some other way—as it has done to the luckiest of us all at one time or another. But while I myself had overcome early discouragements, and my life had led me into healthier and more normal channels, my poor friend had been carried downstream into viciousness and criminality—perhaps perforce of irresistible circumstance. There was a wistful though anguished gleam in his eyes . . . how I wanted to be his friend, to help him. I almost loved the man.

Timidly I reached out to caress his arm.

"I understand," I whispered softly. "I understand and I pity."

A frightful spasm siezed his features. His eyes and forehead and cheek muscles twisted fearfully—as if torn between the two struggling aspects of his character, the Dr. Jekyll and Mr. Hyde of it. I watched with bated breath. But suddenly the battle was determined. The baron's jaw shot out into a hideous rigidity, he drew back his arm, and with the knuckles of his open hand struck me full across the mouth.

"Why, you presumptuous little French bitch!" he hissed deliberately. "So you understand, eh? Well, you understand more than is good for you! And you pity, too? Ha, ha! You pity your omnipotent master, eh? You pity me? Ha, ha, ha! I—who could crush you like a worm—if crushing weren't too short and easy an end for a female so brazen as you. I suppose you were going to reform me, weren't you—you big-hearted, tight-cunted foreign hussy! Well, to show you how close I am to resuming the narrow path of virtue, we shall stage tonight for your especial benefit an orgy such as you have never witnessed before and may not live to witness again. But in the meanwhile, down on your knees, bitch, take this prick between your pretty bleeding lips, and suck for the life of you—for I give you just three minutes by this clock in which to make me spend—and if I don't, may your God help you; I won't wait till tonight but will throttle you here and now!"

His insane fury brooked no protest. I complied—sucking with all my strength and breath as I had never sucked before—sucked and lipped and tongued, though my mouth bled profusely from his inhuman blow—sucked and sucked with all my might, though hot scalding tears ran down my cheeks, tears of rejected kindness, of deepest despair, of forlorn hopelessness. What an impossible, impossible world! Oh, how I wanted to sob and cry out loud and rail at fate's injustices and the imperviousness of human stupidity! But that great detestable prick of his all but choked me.

And all the time this beast that I had almost loved laughed and laughed at me. Laughed—while with both his hands he rained blows upon my head, pulled my hair, pinched and twisted my ears, my breasts, or anything he could lay hands on.

Fairly enough, as he had put it, diabolically enough as the reader will agree, he had allowed his watch to dangle on the front of his vest within my full view, to tantalize and distract me further from this task which so demanded my highest concentration. And now, as the second-hand relentlessly traversed—all too quickly—for the second time its short circular path, denoting the lapse of two-thirds of my allotted time—and that towering master of my fate still showed not the least signs of coming, a cold horror swamped all my being. My jaws and throat were aching unendurably with the strain of my continuous sucking, yet as that mocking indicator rounded its second lap, and without even pausing, started chopping off the fragments of what was to me the last minute of my life—that leering clock face seemed to rush forward like the head of an oncoming railroad engine, filling my entire consciousness, relegating to a far distant and almost imperceptible plane of awareness all my other sensations: the continued torturings of my persecutor's hands, the suffocating bulk of the huge prick that engorged my throat and blocked my respiration. A mad impulse seized me—to arrest at any cost the cruel working of that chronometer—but I seemed no longer to have any volitional control over my body. Louder and louder became the ticking of the clock, more and more urgent, seeming to shriek at me, "Quick! Quick!" Each time it resembled the clang of a sledgehammer, measuring out my doom.

Fifteen, twenty, thirty, forty of the sixtieths of my last minute passed into irretrievability— while all of that fateful clock-dial became shrouded in blackness, except for the remaining segment to be traversed, which glowed with an increasing fiery brilliance that seared into my soul. Quick! quick! The strand of remaining brightness became narrower and narrower, as it was submerged, by the tides of oblivion. Quick! quick! But I could do nothing.

Five! Four! Three seconds remain—and now the clamor of time is earsplitting. Two! The executioner's axe is lifted . . . a sharp convulsing tremor seizes my body . . . all my muscles tense for that final moment—involuntarily my teeth close, without regard for what is between them . . . a roar of equivocal agony from the baron breaks into my tiny microcosm of horror and dispels it, drowning out the awaited final clang and rocketing me

147

instantly into full consciousness. With his great bestial hands locked about my head he holds me from him, pulling his part sharply from my mouth, and as a thick shower of his hot sperm spurts onto my face and bosom, announcing his climax, the villain demonstrates the intensity of his sensations by viciously digging his thumbs into the sensitive nerve-center that exists just above my eyes. I faint away, blinded with the excruciating pain, but soothed by the realization that I am saved—veritably, in the nick of time. Apparently, it was my accidentally biting him that brought on his orgasm. The sadistic, or abnormal delight in the infliction of pain, it seems then, does not necessarily exist as a thing apart from the obverse or masochistic manifestation. It was no doubt sensitivity to pain that made my persecutor so aware an exponent of the effectiveness of another's suffering.

In the evening, the baron did not break his promise. All eight of us were summoned out to suffer for his pleasure, and horror reigned supreme at Feodorovskoe that night. It makes my cunt crawl to think of it even now. Furthest be it from me to try to arouse the reader's pity or incredulity. Similarly distant from my plan is it to mar the general tone and purpose of my book by playing up this unpleasant aspect of my Russian adventures. Yet, not to be accused of concealing too much, and judging that a few pages given over to the abnormal side of sex will not be amiss, convincing the reader, as I trust it will, that he can never be too thankful for the normalcy of his instinct, even if it be qualified by a few personal foibles, so long as they are this side of criminality—I shall describe that typically horrible night; but as unsubjectively, as impersonally as possible.

When we were all assembled, nude of course, our dreaded master appeared, wearing over his usual clothes a coat of thin mesh-steel studded with numerous small metal projections—obviously calculated to make any of us whom he should so honor painfully aware of his embrace. In his hands he carried a varied assortment of knouts and switches, the least dangerous of his devices.

For all of half an hour he amused himself by merely milling us around the room in a circle, like beasts in a cage, while he stood in the center, keeping us on the alert with anything but playful blows on the thighs or buttocks from one or another weapon in his armory. Next he compelled us to jump over stools or chairs at the crack of his whip, helping one of the less agile of us over the hurdles with a vicious kick in the backside, tripping up another with his foot so that she fell face forward to the floor—the villain evidencing great delight at the profuse bleeding that resulted at her nose.

But even these spectacles were all too tame for his overstimulated, jaded senses—and to help work himself into a proper frenzy he would, at frequent intervals, take great lusty swigs of various liquors that he had supplied himself with. Suddenly . . .

"Well, you whores. I think I want to piss," he spoke up.

Instantly all gathered about him and, falling to their knees, offered their mouths as receptacles. Only I, not yet acquainted with the procedure, held back in indignation. Noting this, he kicked aside the others and strode toward me.

"Quite obstinate still, eh?" he muttered. "You have a lot to learn yet around here." And throwing me prone on my back onto the bare floor, he drew out his genito-urinary apparatus, now flaccid and obviously employable only in the latter of its hyphenated capacities, and brought it close to my face.

"But wait"—he suddenly changes his purpose—"I'll show you a different trick." And reaching for a bottle of alcoholic spirits, he takes a long drink of it and then pours the rest over my cunt and pubic hairs, soaking the latter thoroughly. Then, igniting a match, he briefly explains his purpose, in sneering, cynical tones.

"I am going to set fire to your bush," he says fiendishly, "that dear silky clump that lends such a false air of mystery to that pubic slot of yours. Then I will extinguish the fire with this," indicating his drooping member. "But if the sight of your distress moves or arouses me too much, then of course, I won't be able to come to your aid with the liquid that you just spurned. Do you understand?"

I was horrified—but had to conceal the fact —for I knew only too well (from my medical studies if not by experience) that if he should be favored with an erection he would be utterly unable to urinate—and I knew, too, that only my visible suffering could bring about that result.

He approached the burning match to the spirit-soaked delicate forestation of my pubic delta. Immediately it caught fire . . . but to my surprise and relief, I felt no pain. At least, not yet. The alcohol he had poured over me burned with a bright blue flame; but somehow, the considerable residue of water from the spirits protected my skin from the conflagration, and even the hairs themselves were scarcely singed. A miracle indeed, and one comparable to any of those marvels described in the Bible; say those of the prophets who went through fire unscathed, or that of Moses and the burning bush that would not consume itself. But the baron, disappointed at my failure to evince any pain, and realizing that the fire would soon expire of itself, brought his part to bear upon me, and with a good deal more satisfaction, extinguished the conflagration with a copious stream of his urine.

This last procedure seemed to bring the flush of interest to his blood, and soon he was in fine enough fettle to demand and execute more active and direct satisfactions. Not at all flattered or overjoyed was I, however, to be again chosen as his maid of honor, and the recipient of his now monstrous, calloused cock —especially since, before wedging himself into my cunt, he took the precaution of slipping a little metal guard over the upper juncture of the lips and clitoris to ensure that I derived no pleasure from his contacts.

But even with this inhuman limitation effected, he was not yet satisfied to push on to the end of his abominable pleasures. No sooner was he properly in the saddle—to my deep discomfort only—he had his daughter Sonya approach and, squatting over my bo-

151

som, offer her cunt to his mouth—a proceeding most strange indeed since I could see in it only the normal bestowal of joy and not the perverted infliction of pain. But more involved still were the requirements of his diseased imagination—he had four more of the girls lie, two on each side of me, parallel but reverse to each other's nudity—presenting within easy reach of both his hands a choice of either breasts or cunts to caress or torture. The two remaining women, their buttocks raised in the air, had candles inserted in the anus of each. The tapers were lit, and these human candelabra crouched nearby to give additional light to his nefarious procedures.

Then and only then did he start fucking me. And how he fucked me. With full, fierce, bone-breaking shoves he drilled deep into my innards with his brutal bar, deeper and deeper, till its dull head battered heavily against the entrance of my very womb. But he was not entirely into me yet. I could feel that he had inches still to spare. He continued feeding in his cock. It strained and tore at the mouth of my uterus—for my cunt proper is already filled to capacity. If only I hadn't been prohibited from enjoying his fiendish device, the pain would not have been so unendurable. But pain alone was my lot—and at last, to the accompaniment of internal physical pangs comparable only to those of childbirth, the thick head of his seemingly endless prick forced its way through the tiny aperture into the very throbbing womb itself! A third maidenhead was thus taken! I cried unto the gods, demanding to know was there no end to the things that women could suffer at the hands of men! Here I had been thinking that all that could arouse the envy and violence of the male sex had been taken from me—or at least made painlessly accessible—and here was yet another atrocity—and if anything the most excruciating of all—inflicted upon me.

As the climactic frenzy of his criminal pleasures approached and the pain that he caused me alone was insufficient to satisfy the fury of his destructive lust, he scratched and tore at the breasts and privates of the human sacrifices that lay on each side of me. At the same time he bit ferociously and unrestrainedly at the cunt of his beautiful daughter, who was squatting over my face, as I have said. In accord with his philosophizing, it was obvious that his diseased mind required the utmost external testimony to his own perverted cruelty.

At last the prayed-for ending came. I could not have held out much longer. The huge head of his prick, insinuated into my very womb like a burrowing serpent, cast out its prolific load of venom, flooding all of that dangerously susceptible female organ that it had always been my chief care to protect from insemination. Not yet content with soaking me merely in his vital secretions, he ordered Sonya, at the very moment of his orgasm, to void her bladder full upon my neck and breasts. . . but so miserable, abject and pain-wracked was I, that this seemed only the least of his indignities. Indeed, the tepid steady trickle that flowed from between the tortured lips of her darling vulva soothed my pain as would a warm gentle rain from heaven.

Unceremoniously the baron withdrew from my torn distended body and went on to the execution of other brutalities—brutalities in which, fortunately, I played no further part other than that of unwilling spectator—brutalities which I have not the heart to describe, and which were repeated night after night in our captor's den.

On this same evening, though, something occurred to give me a ray of hope—that suggested that there might yet be some interference from the outside world to put an end to our imprisonment. For just as the baron was about to immolate one of our number, Illena, in the fires of his bestiality, there were sounds of a struggle at the door, and despite the two guards that tried to hold him back, in rushed a huge elderly peasant who turned out to be none other than Illena's father, come to wrest her from the suspicious employment that had kept her away from home for some weeks.

Our elation was short-lived however. He was no match for the baron and his men. Soon he was overcome, and with strong ropes trussed up against a pillar, and our master, with the consummate cruelty he was distinguished for, proceeded to rape the peasant's daughter before his very eyes. The old man strained desperately on his bonds to get at the villain, actually frothing at the mouth because of his helplessness and uttering inconceivable oaths and threats. But the baron went right on—fucking the pretty Illena with every ostentation, making all sorts of cynical, taunting remarks to the father, and finally transferring his profanations from her cunt to her backside—to torture the father even more with this vicious demonstration upon the tender body of his beloved daughter. From threats the helpless parent turned to entreaties and prayers, calling upon all the saints and the Virgin Mary to aid him. This seemed only to increase the baron's unholy delight.

"Stop your sanctimonious mouthing, old man!" he said. "If you knew what fine fucking your daughter makes, how tight her cunt and how warm and tighter still her rear sheath is, you would want to try her yourself. I could prove to you, if I wished, that your loud words are the ravings, not of injured innoncence, but of envy—and of a lust deeper than mine in that it considers itself thwarted by the restrictions of man and church. If I were to release you now on condition that you carnally possess the body of your charming offspring, you would be glad of the excuse to commit the incest."

"If you were to release me now," the great muzhik roared through clenched teeth, "I would tear you limb from limb, even if it took my last bit of strength to do it!"

The baron paused in his occupation. A smile of cynical confidence was on his face. He withdrew his still randy member from the tight illicit channel to which it had been paying homage.

"Illena," he ordered, "go and see what you can do with those pretty hands and lips of yours to put your father in a better humor! Many times as a child you have no doubt coveted that which you saw bestowed only on your mother. Here is your chance to get it and satisfy those same desires."

"Sir . . ." Illena stammered through her tears with every determination, "you have compelled me to do many things since I have been here, but I would rather you killed me than force me thus to shame my respected father. Ask anything, but not that . . ."

The baron scowled. From a nearby cupboard he fetched a revolver and leveled it at the breast of the muzhik.

"I hate to do this Illena," he said with frigid calm, "but you leave me no alternative. If I can't make your father one of us by sealing his lips with a sin of his own commission, then I must insure that he does not leave here alive to carry tales abroad . . ."

"Oh no!" Illena screamed, "don't shoot . . . I'll do as you command, sir. But the Lord knows I am innocent. He will forgive me . . ."

And falling to her knees before her father, she tearfully and hesitantly opened his shirt and brought out the reverend instrument of her creation, caressing it, while the baron, whenever her actions lagged, egged her on with pitiless threats. If the mere vision of his daughter's nude beauty had not been enough to make the poor muzhik forget the taboos of his relationship, certainly he would need have been more or less than human to withstand the inescapable seduction of her soft hands and luscious lips.

"No! No! Let him rather kill us both!" he had cried at her first overtures; but now he was sobbing and moaning. "Oh, my dear daughter! My sweet, loving daughter! Oh—you wonderful, beautiful woman!" And with each progression of his locution and her manipulation, it became more and more apparent that in the struggle between the ethicological and the biological, the latter and more fundamental power would soon triumph. Nor was my prediction a mere empty hypothesis: it was substantiated momentarily by the visibly increasing bulk and hardness of the muzhik's great Tartar cock.

The contrition with which the lovely Illena executed the baron's commands could not mitigate their effectiveness. Soon the paternal bludgeon reached that bursting maximum of magnitude which insured that any insurrection of vestigial moral-conscience would be summarily repulsed, and the baron, beckoning to two of the girls, had them raise the form of the tearfully protesting Illena to the level of her father and forcibly join his quivering member to her unwilling cunt . . .

The baron stepped behind the post to which the muzhik was tied, and with a single slash of his knife severed the ropes that bound him.

"Now, old man," he sneered, "you are free to execute your threat of tearing me limb from limb—that is, if you can bring yourself to leave that delicious warm cunt you are now in possession of."

The muzhik looked around him with wild eyes that mirrored his confusion and perplexity. Then he looked down at the pretty tear-streaked face of his daughter, framed in her flowing black hair, looked at her soft undulating bosom, shaken by her frightened sobs, and then lower still, over her bare white belly to the dark shaded mount of love where her body was connected to his through the medium of his immense penile peninsula . . . a veritable "bridge of sighs." He groaned; and in that groan was epitomized all his horror, despair, resignation, desire—and yes, pleasure —then, slipping his now free hands to the white luxuriousness of his daughter's buttocks and drawing her whole body fiercely to him to keep from getting dislodged, he rammed himself further up into her tender body, and sank down with her to the floor. Negotiating the fall without losing an inch or a moment's contact with her exquisite female flesh, he proceeded at once to fuck her with a fury and lust that was, if anything, only augmented by the illicit incestuousness of their carnal connection.

"Father, Father! Are you mad?" the horrified Illena screamed, struggling to get away; but the now brutish parent pinned her down with his mass, and soon it became obvious that she was being vanquished by that inescapable potent charmer of his.

"Think of Mother . . . oh!" she gasped in a last appeal to his conscience. But if he thought of Mother, it was no doubt to decide how much nicer daughter was. And if *she* thought of Mother, it was now probably to think of what Mother was missing—for her desperate wrigglings were now becoming heaves of passionate cooperation . . . For all of its inevitability, I was horrified. Rape was bad enough. But to have the daughter thus join in with a will on the incest was too much. Whatever remaining belief I may have had in the efficacy of man's laws and arrangements, I lost it then. Only this remained: that prick is prick and cunt is cunt, and ever the twain shall meet.

And so father and daughter continued their

lustful, maddened mingling of flesh and blood with one's own flesh and blood, of kind with kind, the daughter wrapping her little but richly developed white thighs and shapely calves tensely about her father's loins, her bottom working wildly—the parent plunging back and forth into the hot moist flesh of the cunt he had fathered—both of them gasping words of pleasure and endearment that were not at all the usual expressions of filial and paternal respect that one might expect between such close relations. It was soon over—that most proscribed of all prohibitions, the inspersion of a father's seed into the womb of his offspring —with no bolts from heaven to evidence the Divine wrath—only sighs and moans of ecstasy, wild quivering of lustful pleasure, and then the final orgasmic transports, the crucial stiffening, the relaxation.

For a time they lay together. I could picture the tragic turmoil that must have existed in the mind of each. At last they shuddered, guiltily avoiding each other's eyes. The father slunk off into a corner, as if to hide himself from all the world, his head hung low in shame. Even the baron must have realized, if not been touched by, his anguish—for he came out of his cynical gloating for a moment to slap him on the back and say:

"Cheer up, old man. Cunt is cunt—so don't let the accident of your relationship trouble you. I'll give you a crack at my own daughter if you wish, just to even accounts. But first I'll fuck her myself—to show you that you're not the only father in this district who doesn't allow the law to frighten him off the cunt he's most entitled to. What do you say, eh?"

The muzhik did not reply. The baron shrugged his shoulders indifferently and left him, impatient to himself again execute the crime the sight of which had just rearoused his interest.

A moment later was the deafening report of a gun being fired. Even before the dense smoke lifted, we saw the bleeding form of Illena's father crumpling to the floor. He had taken the revolver which the baron had earlier left carelessly on the sideboard and had shot himself through the heart.

"Old fool!" the baron muttered, and resumed his interrupted sexual calisthenics.

A few weeks after this tragic incident, as I was walking along a corridor that led past the baron's private study. I was arrested by the sound of an altercation within, in which my name was unmistakably mentioned.

"So you're not going to give me even a single crack at that little French Madeleine of yours?" I recognized the voice of Ivan, the man who had brought me to this hateful place.

"No!" the baron answered definitely with an oath. "Here's one female that I like well enough to keep to myself. Why her tight oily slot milks me in one half the time the others take. No! I've paid you for her, haven't I? Well, she's mine!"

"A fine friend you are, Grigor. Getting exclusive, aren't you?"

"No, Ivan. But why have it stretched any more than necessary? I've offered you your pick of all my other women. You can even have my daughter if you wish."

"Damn you, Grigor. I don't go in for children—and least of all could I copulate with the spawn of any cursed devil like you!"

The baron laughed complacently, while Ivan angrily continued.

"I brought you the French girl, didn't I—the nicest piece of flesh you ever had. If I hadn't, you wouldn't have her. It may have been your money, but it was my personality, my time and effort that got her here. If you can't treat me honestly, you can go out and trap your own cunt hereafter. I'm through!" And he came stalking out the door.

"Don't forget tonight, Ivan," the baron called after him good-naturedly. "You're still invited, you know. And if you don't want Sonya, there's still Olga, and Grushenka, and . . ."

Ivan slammed the door, scowling fiercely. But when he spied me, his face lighted up. He drew me aside into a little alcove and reached hungrily within my dressing gown for the opulent curves of my nude body, of which he no doubt still had pleasant recollections.

"With or without his consent," he muttered, as if speaking only to himself, "I'll fuck her anyway!"

"Don't I have anything to say about that?" I whispered coquettishly, narrowing my eyes as if amorously and running my fingertips lightly up his thighs.

Silently he crushed me in his arms. Then, slipping one hand between our bodies, and pinching the full lips of my vagina as if to reassure himself that they were still there after his two months absence, he proceeded to bring out his quite sensibly stiffened love-part.

Against my smooth bare skin I could feel the delicious heat emanating from his smoldering boulders.

"Listen to me, Ivan!" I whispered hurriedly, replacing his thick hot organ within his trousers and rebuttoning them with some difficulty, "it would be madness to take me now. The baron is likely to come upon us at any moment. You must wait—and you will have *everything*. I want it as badly as you; the baron has been giving me nothing but pain. Do you want more such nights of love as we spent together on the train—and that night in the hotel at Ekaterinodar? Then get me away from this horrible madhouse. No, no, Ivan—please don't take it out again . . . there . . . now he'll stay put. Listen. This is neither the time nor the place for it, Ivan. Get me out of here and you may have me for as long as you wish—a whole month even—and I'll refuse you nothing."

His obvious reluctance to forego the present gradually gave way to eager anticipation of the future that I pictured for him so glowingly.

"Agreed!" he finally said hoarsely, squeezing both the cheeks of my posteriors in friendly renunciation. "This very night it shall be! Leave everything to me." And he hurried away, chuckling to himself at the thought of how he would avenge the baron's parsimoniousness.

I awaited the evening's orgy with great anxiety. Would he be there or not? He was—and the baron, pleased to have his invaluable recruiting officer still with him, was in extraordinary good humor, tossing off glass after

162

glass of vodka and entertaining his friend with loud vulgar jokes. I watched Ivan closely. He seemed to have forgotten all about me and was diddling around with one of the other girls. But during a moment's diversion, I saw him stealthily empty a powder into the baron's glass. The baron went on drinking. Soon he declared he was getting sleepy. Then he complained of dizziness. A moment later, he collapsed to the floor in a sodden stupor.

Ivan was equal to the occasion. "You, Madeleine," he called to me in a loud voice, "run and send the doormen in here! Tell them their master's ill. Call the outside guard, too." And in a whisper, and in French, so that none but I might understand, "Wait for me behind the cart out there . . ."

"And all you other chattering females," he roared masterfully, "get back to your rooms at once!"

I rushed out and did as I had been directed. The guards did not think to doubt my word, but left their posts hurriedly to go to their master. Outside I drew my first breath of freedom's air. In the pitch dark, I had some difficulty finding the cart, but succeeded finally, and hid under a quantity of straw and some robes. A few minutes later I was joined by Ivan, who had left ostensibly to fetch a doctor. My absence had not been noted yet.

All night long we drove in our slow vehicle, my anxiety gradually subsiding as the mileage between ourselves and the castle increased and no pursuers came after us. No doubt it must have been well into the next day before my flight was discovered.

Suffice it to say that we escaped—although

I was actually without even a chemise—having nothing but my kimona to my back. Need I record, too, that as soon as we were a safe number of hours away from my prison and before the dawn broke, Ivan joined me in the straw for a half-hour of relaxation? And must I remind the inquisitive reader that it had been over two months since I had really had a piece—to convince him of the glorious fuck my saviour gave me and the superb belly-bumping I returned, pouring out at last the pent-up passions of months?

With this supremely satisfying spend—in the straw of a cart in the south of Russia—with the dawn breaking over the yellow hills of the Caucasus—let me draw the curtain and bring to an end this longest and perhaps most trying episode in my life and in my book.

# CHAPTER NINE

Let me pass rapidly over the succeeding weeks. Of course, when we reached Ekaterinodar, the rail terminus, Ivan had my wardrobe temporarily replenished with some quaint but becoming Russian costumes. My first act, as soon as I was able to appear upon the streets was to hasten to the post office, where, at the *poste restante* I found many anxious letters from Fleurette and others awaiting me. I immediately telegraphed messages of reassurance to Paris and requisitions for more sophisticated apparel.

From there, Ivan and I journied to Yalta, a fashionable Russian resort in the semitropical Crimea, near Sebastopol. Here we spent three delightful weeks together that were for me vacation, dissipation and recuperation—all rolled into one—and most of it taken in bed . . . on my back. Apart from Ivan, nothing particular transpired, except a brief affair with a handsome young army officer that covered just two stolen afternoons. And, oh yes—come to think of it—another with a charmingly impatient young bellboy at the hotel, who discovering my infidelity to my registered protector, exacted from me some pleasant enough blackmail in the form of two or three wee little pushes—the price of his silence.

Something else, however, that weighed on my conscience much more heavily, was a secret little experiment that makes me blush still when I think of it, and which I could heretofore bring myself to divulge only to these tolerant, incensorious blank pages before me.

Ivan, as is the custom with many traveling Russians, had brought with him a large handsome wolfhound whom he called Yosh—perhaps the equivalent of Josh. Rarely was he without him. In fact, the dog was even permitted to share our apartment—and many a time, as Ivan and I lay writhing in amorous combat, he would sit alongside watching sagely, with his great red tongue lolling moistly from his spread jaws—or he would pace nervously up and down at the foot of the bed, now and then throwing quizzical glances at us, as if wondering whether he should interfere to save his master, or as if perhaps awaiting his turn . . .

One warm lazy afternoon when Ivan had gone out alone, leaving Yosh asleep on the rug, I came out of my cool bath all dripping wet and crossed the bedroom in search of a towel. I must have shaken some drops of cold water on the dog, for he awoke, shook himself in turn and followed me about the room with a hungry docility that was entirely out of keeping with his usual fierce and unfriendly character. As I finished drying and threw myself luxuriatingly upon a couch to rest, he came up alongside and unexpectedly nestled his moist and slightly feverish nose in the palm of my hand, as if inviting my caresses. I was startled; but pleasantly so. Nothing other than the soft mushy nose of a dog against the sensitive palm of a woman could produce the lush tickling little thrill that I experienced. What would it feel like elsewhere, I could not help thinking . . . In my investigations around Paris, I had seen such things, and had been slightly repelled thereby. But here, in the intimacy and loneliness of my chamber, with the actual medium of experimentation before me, and with the blinds drawn, the whole matter assumed an entirely different aspect. What harm could there be? It must be strange . . . different . . .

Yosh, meanwhile, was nuzzling and sniffing over my whole body. The double touch of his nose and tongue on and about my breasts and nipples, my abdomen, my thighs, was beginning to drive me mad with perverse curiosity and lubriciousness. As his keen sniffling led him inevitably toward that vital juncture whose processes, no matter how recently combated by the hygiene of bathing, work always to produce faint sensual aromas to attract members of the opposite sex, be they of whatever species, I began slowly to spread my thighs . . . but a sudden fear arrested me. What if in his abandoned fury the animal should bite me? I could not risk having that essential part of me put out of commission. . . I jumped up from my reclining position, and from Ivan's trunk, hurriedly fetched a leather muzzle that Yosh had to wear whenever on the promenade, and adjusted it on his head so that he could open his jaws enough to dangle his tongue, but not enough to bite . . .

Back to the couch I went, the great panting beast close beside me. This time I myself directed his head to the region of my mount of Venus, throwing my thighs wide apart, burying and rubbing his damp, spongy nose between the gaping lips of my vulva, which I held open with my fingers to aid him.

"Lick, Yosh!" I whispered, quartering my pink cleft to the utmost—and incredibly, the dog seemed to understand. His long red soft rag of a tongue came out and wiped awkwardly across my sensitive cunt membranes. By my caresses and rebukes, I rewarded his successes and punished his wanderings, till at last he acquired the proper knack. True, the hound once made an effort to mount me with his whole body, and I had a most violent time restraining him and putting him back in his place; but soon his tongue was again stroking away at my whole cunt and clitty as only a tongue made for lapping can do.

I came very quickly. The very inhuman quality, if not the unconsciousness of the agency, acted like a quirt upon my passions. It was incomparable. Yet, as the pleasure of the climax faded, I could not help but feel ashamed of the bestiality of the act—innocent enough though it was in fact, since neither the dog nor I was harmed by it. But I still had my canine lover to contend with. He kept climbing upon me and rubbing his stiff red-brown sex part against my bare thighs for the satisfaction he had bestowed and now wanted for himself. Earlier in the incident I would not have hesitated to relieve him with my fingers. I might even have allowed him to mount and enter me in the regular manner, if I had not been even then somewhat repelled by the unpleasant dark hairiness of his organ and attracted by the novelty of my original project. But now, with my own end attained, and a little disgusted withal, as I have said, I kept fighting him off. The beast became threateningly ferocious—and finally I had to ring for a servant and have him taken away. Only then did I realize that in my nefarious excitement I had actually forgot to lock my door . . . I had indeed done a risky thing. Ivan was much puzzled by the dog's strange conduct toward me thereafter. I did not tell him that the hound had "smelled cunt" in the fullest sense of the words.

At about this time—and for the first time in my career—I was troubled by an unpleasant discovery. A certain date of this month came and went without the appearance of my menstrual flow. I was pregnant—the baron's fierce internal onslaught had done it for me. He had forbidden any of us the use of contraceptive devices, and even if I had employed one, it could not have been able to withstand the rough treatment he had subjected me to. But no sentimentalities of accepting the unwelcome state of motherhood did I entertain—and the reader least of all will blame me for declining to foster the fruit of the detestably perverted baron's rape.

Ivan, when he heard of my predicament, considerately agreed to cut short the period of our liaison. I hurried back to Paris and consulted my doctor. It was an even simpler matter than I had expected, this process of expelling an inseminated ovum. Tampons of gauze were gently packed into my womb and were allowed to expand overnight. In the morning when they were removed, the undesirable substances came with them. The worst that I had to endure was the equivalent of a mild tummy ache—and certainly this was nothing compared to the pains of even the most fortunate childbearing. Moreover, while my slight discomfort signified the end of an unpleasant situation, the pangs of sustaining nature's cruelest process in giving birth to a child mean only the beginnings of trouble. Much, if not all of the widespread fear of abortion is, like most popular impressions, due to the untruthful propaganda of churchmen and governments, each bent on getting the greatest possible number of recruits for their respective causes, whether ecclesiastic or secular.

Back to the fucking once more, the entire nightmare of my Russian adventures was soon forgotten in one continual round of pleasure. My absence had, if such a thing were possible, increased my popularity tenfold. All my past lovers came back enbloc for reengagements— as if they had all been saving it for me —which was of course not very likely. As usual, I would skim or sip a bit of their top cream and pass them right on to my assistants for the more arduous and prolonged milking. But now my faithful little squad of Fleurette, Suzanne and Manon was far too small to cope with the vigorous platoon of pricks that presented themselves nightly at our private parties for immediate immersion in soft flesh. With all the calculation in the world, temporal, physiological, geometrical, equational and fractional, we couldn't accommodate them all. All we succeeded in doing was cluttering our books with future engagements that we could never catch up with, or postponing an admirer so injudiciously that he finally required triple our time to assuage him.

There was but one way to relieve the increasing congestion and that was to strengthen our ranks with fresh enlistments. This I did—carefully and critically, having the finest flesh marts of the world to choose from.

Unwillingly I was being drawn by force of irresistible circumstance into the capacity of professional "entremetteuse." Much as I struggled against the commercialization of a "métier" which, I assure the reader, I had chosen only because it embodied my cardinal success, how one friend always insists on bringing another friend, how impossible it is to refuse one's hospitality to a stranger when he has charm, wealth, and all other attributes that obtain admission to our house for so many others—how, in brief, the moving snowball gathers size and weight till it is an avalanche that cannot be stayed.

Before long there were 14 of us. Because of the liberality of my terms and the generosity of my patrons, there were always scores of girls from all walks of life on my waiting list, anxious to fight under my aegis in the tender tournaments of love. Again and again I was assured that never had Paris been honored by a *maison de plaisir* quite so nice, refined and discreet as mine since the days of Madame Giordan (who, operating an establishment for princes and bishops back in the 18th century, could scarcely be considered serious competition). Only in this respect did I differ from that other famous Madame: I never accepted the service of genuine virgins. The applicant could go home and snip her maidenhead with mother's sewing scissors, she could try sliding violently down the banisters (as so many respectable women manage to have done by the time they reach their nup-

tial bed), or more sensibly still, entrust the
delicate operation of some worthy stiff-pronged
boyfriend; but always and absolutely I refused to be instrumental in the actual "making up her mind" or launching of her career.
Frequently too I would make them undergo a
sort of noncommittal apprenticeship, during
which they would serve as waitresses or
maids. Since the rules of my house strictly
forbade patrons molesting the help in any
way, they were given every decent opportunity to watch everything that went on, themselves untouched, and then they could decide
whether or not they really wished to enter
my services as true dispensers of joy. Because of this particular conscientiousness of
mine, I was rewarded by a congratulatory
letter from the Prefect of Police, in which he
authorized me to frame and exhibit a testimony to the fact that my house did not
countenance that one sexual offense that the
French law forbids, the seduction of virgins
and minors.

Frequent medical examinations under my
personal supervision were, even at the beginning, a strict part of our regimen. Should a
girl be found infected, which due to our hygienic precautions was nigh impossible and
happened only to two of my girls in all the
years of our association, she was immediately retired until she could present a totally
negative Wasserman reaction and a 100 per
cent clear bill of health. I take greatest pride
in boasting that, inconceivable as it may
seem to those fearful prudes who are ignorant of the aseptic immaculacy that reigns in
the high-class Parisian house of accommo-

dation today, I can truthfully say that my establishment and my girls have never even once been instrumental in the transmission of any venereal disease. It follows without exaggeration then that mine was the kind of place where no patron need hesitate to go down on—or even drink our health from—the cunny of any one of us—which was at all times as kissable and clean as the lips of his wife or sweetheart—if not considerably more so.

From the foregoing prospectus I must pray the reader *not* to conclude two things: first, that we did all the fucking in Paris. We did not. Paris is a big place, and fucking, thank God, is not restricted by law here, or by patent or copyright anywhere. Secondly, I would not have the reader think for one moment that I allowed the increasing burdens of my generalship to interfere with my own active participation in the delights of Venus—for when indeed has wholesaling prevented profitable "retailing" on the side? Fleurette made a competent second in command—and whenever my cunt called me into the thick of battle or into some private hand-to-hand duel, whenever too I was exhausted by some too furious engagement, she was always there to uphold the standard in my stead, as gracious and well-poised a hostess as I, with the advantage, if anything, of a cool prepossession which was not always mine when in the presence of prick. Never more than once in a night did she allow her white shoulder to go to the mat in the delicious wrestle of love—and so, must I confess it, she had more time to attend to my routine affairs than I was willing to afford them myself.

Another problem that I was confronted with at this time: the expensiveness of our usual champagne dinners and parties of necessity barred many friends who, while eminently worthy, were somewhat limited in purse. Many fascinating young artists and writers were found in this category. I did not like to forego the benefit of their company. There was but one thing to do. I opened a branch establishment of more modest pretensions on the Left Bank, on the Boul' Mich', and divided my time between the two places, riding to and fro in the luxurious Hispana-Suiza that I had recently acquired—and indeed, more frequently than not, giving the greater part of my time (and not time only) to the stimulating long-haired Bohemians that gathered at my less expensive resort. Times without number I would generously spread my thighs for no other stipend than the gift of a canvas or sketch by some then unknown post-impressionist painter, and soon every available inch of wall-space in my Latin Quarter house was covered with some such offering. Surprisingly and gratifyingly enough, many of these apparently meaningless and worthless pictures, earned by a few ungrudging motions of my hips years ago, have since the war become much sought after masterpieces that have netted me thousands of francs.

One must not think, however, that with the increasing systemization of my lovelife all adventure came to an end. Not at all. The life of a courtesan in itself is the most varied and interesting occupation, indisputably, that a woman is capable of following. Add to this my financial independence, and you will agree

174

that whenever things threatened to become at all tiresome, I could very well vary the routine.

Thus, on warm summer evenings, we would sometimes transfer our activities to the shaded groves of the Bois du Boulogne or to one of the other suburban parks. Here, under the moon's indulgent beams and on the soft carpet of the grass we would, with a select group from our clientele, celebrate Priapic rites in the classic manner of the ancient Greeks and Romans. It is really inconceivable how the beauties of the night and the freedom of the open air can make even of the most commonplace fucking an entirely new and dazzling aesthetic experience. What gorgeous dances and lascivious exhibitions my girls, stripped to the nude, would stage for us within the circle of our automobile headlights! And then, the delicious personal relief from all this appetizing stimulation when we scattered in pairs into the woods for the next, but not necessarily the final act of our wondrous drama of the sexes!

At about this time too I met a wealthy motion picture producer who insisted on immortalizing me, as he put it, in some films to be made privately at his Neuilly studios. I had never considered acting as one of my abilities; but if the only acting was fucking, I thought, I certainly had every right to deem myself capable. It was not all quite as simple as that.

At the studio, I was introduced to the handsome fellow who was to play the masculine lead opposite (or atop of) me, and after some scanty instructions from the director, we got right down to business. Beneath the glare of the klieg lights and with the loud clicking of the cameras for accompaniment, my partner proceeded to the preliminaries of courtship with such unhurried finesse and artistry that soon I forgot completely that we were making movies, and became so aroused that I was on the verge of taking the intiative myself. When he had at last finished undressing me deliberately, piece by piece, and with all the provocativeness in the world, he stretched me on the sofa and spent at least ten minutes more and 500 feet of film in placing long, deft, searching kisses in all the tender depressions of my body.

"Fine! Fine!" the director was muttering, hopping excitedly from one leg to the other. "Hurry up! No, no! I mean take it slow and easy. We'll be able to make a ten reeler out of it. Fine! Fine! Now come over her—easy now . . . that's it. Be gentle. Remember—in the script she's supposed to be a virgin—so don't frighten her. That's it! Now—produce the pin. Slide it up her thighs slowly. No! no! *Sacre dieu!* Over to the other side more! How do you expect the cameraman to get her cunt with your big arse blocking the whole set! That's better. Now, hold yourself high—separate the lips of her twat—bring up just the head—rub it around the vulva closer. Good. Now, start shoving in. But slowly! You're going to take her cherry. It's blocked! It's tight! You shove, you push! But remember—you can't get in!"

"That's a damned lie!" I wanted to scream. My hot cunt could have swallowed him in a single quicksand suction of its own, if my partner had not been so bent on teasing me. Millimeter by millimeter, with a stinginess that was scarcely human, he fed his part into my hungry cavity. It seemed to be taking him years; but at last he was all of halfway in. I would have shoved up to meet him—instructions to lie still be damned—had he not held my hips down with his hands and the weight of his body. What a conceited fool of a man, I thought, to be so able to subordinate his instincts to his acting. As for me, I have already recorded how in the presence of prick I lose all presence of mind.

He was halfway in, as I have said, and I was all tensed with dreams of pleasurable possibilities, when suddenly the voice of the director broke in again.

"Now you can't get any further. It's too tight! It hurts her, it's killing her. Now withdraw and take some vaseline from that jar beside you!"

As if vaseline were necessary! I don't know what restrained me from quitting there and then. And now the whole rigimarole had to be gone through again . . . but don't let me torture the reader as my partner tortured me. At last he got it substantially all the way in, the full torrid length of my oily sheath.

"Now rest awhile—as if from a terrific task. Lie still—both of you. Now pull out a little. In again. Very, very slowly! It's too tight still to go any faster."

The teasing was more than I could bear. "If this is entirely for the movies," I muttered sarcastically to my partner, "I guess it'll have to be all right. But if any of this is for me, I wish you'd go just a little bit faster."

"But madame! The director?" he whispered dutifully.

"Oh, fuck the director!" I replied, forgetting myself entirely, "I have my own ideas of the way this should be done!" And dislodging his hands by sheer force from my insatiate hips *I* began fucking him, fast and furiously.

"*Sacre Sainte Ciboire!*" came the direction. "Slow down! *Nom de Dieu!* You'll register nothing but a blur on the film!" But by now neither of us was in a state to pay much heed. My hips were moving at the rate of a hundred oscillations a minute. My lead was plunging his piston at least seventy a minute —making a combined frequency of 170 per. Perhaps we did spoil the film; but thank God, we didn't spoil the fuck.

As I washed up and rested prior to taking the next scene, the director, somewhat appeased by now, approached me.

"Not so bad after all," he grumbled, "but why didn't you at least keep your face toward the cameras and smile when I told you to?"

"I couldn't keep my head still in any one position," I explained simply, "and as for smiling to the cameras, I didn't know where they were, for I went stone blind toward the end. And anyway, I didn't hear a word you shouted."

For the next scene, I was supposed to be alone in my boudoir, examining some erotic postcards and playing with myself, when another male character, who has been watching me through the keyhole, is supposed to burst in and rape me. I carried off my solitary role to perfection, lazily titillating the proud nipple of my right breast, gradually working my hand downward to my mount of love, and finally spreading wide the lips of my cunt to have them photograph to best advantage. During all this the rest of the company stood on the sidelines, watching my performance with tense interest. The dapper moustachioed little gentleman who was to come in next waited eagerly for his cue.

Action was halted a moment for some further instructions, and then the director, with a signal to my second partner to rush in on the set, yelled, "All ready? Shoot!" This last was of course for the cameraman; but my partner must have misunderstood. He did—prematurely, and all over my thighs. I had played my part all too effectively—the delay had been more than he could withstand. The director, in a fury, ordered the film to be chopped and came downstage to give him a good sound word-dressing. This only confused the poor fellow further and made it additionally difficult for him to get in shape to continue the action.

"Come now!" roared the director, "suppose you show us whether or not you can get it in properly before we waste anymore film on you."

All flustered, and blushing furiously, the young man climbed over me and awkwardly brought himself down between the accommodating luxuriousness of my separated thighs.

"*Par dieu!* That's no way to do it!"

groaned the director, tearing his hair in despair.

"Well, supposing you do it yourself!" sighed the martyred thespian with some exasperation.

"I won't *do* it," roared the director, putting aside his megaphone and unbuttoning himself, "but I can show you how it *ought* to be done!" And bringing out a lusciously large tool that immediately upped my respect for the man considerably, he angrily took his position and shoved himself into me with demonstrative unhesitancy.

"There you are!" he said, "do it that way, and not as if you were fumbling in the dark." And immediately he started withdrawing to resume his directorial role. With a little clasp of my moist, velvety sheath I tried to hold him back. So absorbed was he in his work, however, that he didn't seem to notice it, didn't even relax his frown to favor me with an appreciative smile.

"And what am *I* to do in this part?" I queried sweetly.

"Just what you're doing right now: nothing."

"I'm afraid I don't have it straight yet. Do you mind showing me again?"

Grudgingly he complied, returning his loving rigidity to my internal custody once more.

"Don't you think I ought to do *this?*" I asked, giving a brief back and forth movement to my hips.

"No!" he replied sternly.

"Or this?" I gave a little sideways twist to my buttocks. "Or this?" And I gave a slow, sinuous spiral movement to my whole lower body that bestowed upon his flexible rod a membraneous caress that immediately deprived him of all his aloof impersonality.

"Well, maybe," he muttered confusedly.

"And wouldn't you like to play the masculine lead to me hereafter?" I cooed coquettishly, playing my cunt muscles deftly up and down the full length of his instrument.

He squirmed uncomfortably—then squirmed again with reluctant pleasure. Then, suddenly remembering the numerous people who stood by, he glanced officiously at his wrist watch.

"It's time to quit," he shouted irritably. "Company's dismissed. We film again at 10 a.m. tomorrow. And I'll fire anybody who's late!"

As the group of players and employees filed out of the studio and the director turned his attention fiercely and resentfully to me once more, a funny little cameraman, wearing a cap with the visor behind his neck, winked to me significantly. I winked back.

When our little tête-à-tête was over (alas that it was not filmed, for the real thing was much more convincing than any mere acting could be) and I stood in my flimsy chemise slipping my dress over my head prepratory to leaving, I asked him whether I would be satisfactory.

"No!" he rumbled, "you were awful. You'll have to do it all over again. Come in at 9 o'clock tomorrow for some preliminary rehearsal!"

"Will Monsieur ——, my lead, be on hand that early?" I asked sweetly.

He slapped my buttocks mock-angrily—an intimacy that ordinarily I greatly resent—and for the first time yet, laughed heartily.

181

# CHAPTER TEN

I was telling the reader how far from un-interesting my life was, even at this compar-atively sedentary period of my career. In the spring of 1914, Monsignor X, a Papal legate to Paris whom I had met on a number of occasions and who had expressed himself ex-tremely well pleased with my discretion, ap-proached me with a mysterious proposition. The events which followed I now divulge for the very first time. I was to select four of my most trustworthy and attractive girls, and, under a pledge of secrecy, accompany him to Rome on a mission of whose exact nature we were for the time to remain ignorant. Wholly apart from the generous stipend in-volved, I accepted immediately. Within a short time we were transported to the Eternal City and put up at a rather shabby *albergo* fac-ing the muddy River Tiber. As it turned out, we were the sole occupants.

On the second evening after our arrival, our conductor appeared, and taking us down to the cellar of our hotel, led us into a long subterranean tunnel. The damp, dripping walls immediately suggested to me the hypothesis that we were passing under the river to the nearby Castle Angelo, the island stronghold of the Pope. I have since learned definitely that this island, known as the Isola Sacra, is con-nected by passages under the river with the Vatican Palace on the opposite bank, and is supposed to be resorted to by the Vatican in-mates as a kind of fort in case of military or counter-inquisitional stress.

After passing innumerable ancient doors by

dint of much unbolting of bars and rattling of chains—all of which lent to our adventure a most authentically medieval flavor—we climbed a steep stone stairway and found ourselves suddenly in a sumptuously furnished apartment brightly illuminated by hundreds of candles.

As our eyes became better accustomed to the light, we were confronted by a group of middle-aged, important looking men, clad in clerical garb. They seemed to be awaiting us impatiently. The center of the group, and the particular object of their respects, seemed to be an elderly gentleman who of them all alone remained seated on a regally cushioned dais. Irreligious as I was, I could not help but tremble at the exciting and flattering supposition that flashed through my mind. . .

But we were soon put at our ease. Introductions, obviously false, were made all around: "This is Cardinal Aquaviva, Bishop Cacambo, meet Miss Cunnegonde, here we have Monsignor Farniente," and so on.

As a civilized preliminary to what we had every right to expect, we all retired to an adjoining chamber where a regal repast was spread for us. Each gentleman chose for himself a companion to his taste, and as I was the mistress of my party, I was delegated to the attentions of the elderly gentleman, beside whom I took my place at the table. There was a surplus of males present, but these proceeded to make themselves pleasant and useful in whatever way they could.

As bottle after bottle of rarest old Chianti, muscatel, and lacrimae Christi bubbled forth its contents into our glasses and was tossed under the board to make room for other wines, our party warmed up more and more, the conversation becoming less and less delicate. My priestly companion alone ate and drank with great moderation, and while he made no contribution to the general levity, he would smile indulgently at each lewd sally.

"It is well that they enjoy the relaxations of this earth occasionally, my daughter," he addressed me in his soft kindly voice, "for tomorrow they go forth again to shoulder the cares of both this world and the next." And as if to keep our conversation on a level different from that which went on about us, he spoke to me, not in the bad French which the others employed as an excuse for license, but in a musical crystal-clear Italian that made me glad I had studied enough of this beautiful language to enable me to converse with this great man.

But at this point we were distracted by a great burst of laughter which acclaimed the exploit of one of the cardinals, who unlacing Fleurette's bodice and releasing her luscious little pent-up breasts, placed a kiss deep down between them. Immediately Monsignor R. jumped up, and snatching a dainty slipper from one of her tiny feet, filled it with champagne and gallantly proceeded to drink a toast to her quivering charms. Forthwith all the cavaliers followed suit, first undoing the waists and brassieres of their partners till the table seemed surrounded by a flock of snow-white doves arrested in flight, and then pledging flattering toasts all around.

Not even I was spared—for one of the clerics who was without a partner, seeing my bosom in a state of veiled mystery, came toward me, exclaiming:

"What manner of heresy is this, mademoiselle, that you are permitted to still profane your God-given charms with sinful trappings? With your permission, Reverend Sir, I will strip the applicant of her earthly vestments and prepare her for the communion to come."

Blushing helplessly I looked toward my august partner. He nodded his head, smiling. "You may proceed, Your Eminence." In a moment my bosom too was bared to the excited gaze of all present—and each nipple, in unison no doubt with all the other erectile tissue in that gathering, arose and hardened into a delectable little strawberry. The prelate could not resist the temptation to run his hand over the soft intoxicating curves of my flesh; but the further savoring of them he had to leave to another. Apologizing to my partner, he withdrew for the time.

The earlier awe that my girls and I may have felt at our introduction to this august assembly was by this time, it is needless to state, entirely dissipated. And why not? For whatever our hosts may have been at all other times, it was obvious that tonight they were to be merely human. And their priestly vestments, while perhaps still a restraint upon some of us, would not, I now felt certain, remain in evidence much longer.

We all waited expectantly for something further to be done to crack what little ice may have been unthawed by now. Suddenly, one of the gentlemen, more flushed with drink than the rest, leaping onto the table and dragging my sweet little Gisele after him, proceeded to strip her of her remaining clothes. At his request, a deep armchair was passed up to him, and upon this Gisele threw herself. Reclining far back and spreading wide her adorable, richly-developed thighs, she awaited her lord's pleasure. Snatching up a bottle of champagne and falling to his knees within the grateful haven of her shapely limbs he with one hand gently parted the luscious silk-grown lips of her cunt—which for all the world resembled the inside of a rich casket of dark soft velvet lined with rose-colored satin—and pouring the bubbling contents of the bottle over her mount of Venus, then drank it up as it flowed from the lower end of the channel formed by her widespread vulva.

We all applauded heartily. But when, having sucked up the last drop of the effervescent liquid, he still continued with his mouth at her cunt, and it became clear to us that they intended going through a gamahuching, our enfevered senses broke all bounds of patience. Leaving those two to their devices, we trailed into the other room, some of the girls hopping along in but a single slipper and dragging some already discarded bit of clothing after them, the men with flushed faces and eager mien fingering great threatening (or should I say promising) bulges in the front of their cassocks and pontifical robes.

Then the fierce fun began in real earnest. Manon, with wild sparkling eyes, made a rush for one of the divans, tearing off her remaining clothes even as she made for it. Throwing herself upon the springly furniture, she bounced her superbly rounded buttocks impatiently up and down, screaming, "Come on—anybody—fuck me quick!" I was both proud and a little ashamed of her.

Spreading her legs and opening the lips of her luscious slit, she invited the immediate onslaught of the first comer—and had not long to wait.

In a moment my other girls too were stripped to their skins. Couples sought divans or chairs, or simply sank to the floors that were heavily rugged. Cassocks were thrown back over shoulders or furled up hastily, and monster members that had not tasted female flesh for Lord knows how long came into evidence—only to be quickly hidden away in the hot rosy depths of the clefts that their stiff bursting strength rudely divided.

All this happened ere I was scarcely seated on the platform beside my distinguished consort. The lustful fury that pervaded the room reached even to our little Olympus. Breathing a bit feverishly, I looked inquiringly at my partner. He smiled benignly and made a timid gesture toward my nerve-tautened, swelling breasts; but it was only to cover them with the waist that I still had partially about my shoulders. He was saying something, but I did not hear him, for my attention was now everywhere else: on the moist seething state of my own cunt among other things. However, though a number of the unoccupied men were casting longing eyes at me, none made any move to rescue me from their superior. So I tried to make the best of it. Uncovering my bosom once more, I cupped one of my swelling white globes alluringly in one hand and slipped my other hand under the folds of the reverend sir's robe, in search of the proof of his manhood. He arrested me gently but firmly, and with a sad smile said:

"Whether happily or unhappily, I am, and have for a long time been, beyond the tyrannical claims of the flesh. If I am here tonight, it is, strangely enough, to cooperate not acutally but morally with my brethren of the stole. I would rather share in their sin, if sin it be and if sin they must, than have them sin without my knowledge and behind my back. In the great and holy task that we are about, it is of all things most essential that there be complete harmony, frankness and understanding between my colleagues in the Lord and myself—else all would indeed be impossible. One lie, one concealment, and they would be forever lost to me and to our cause.

"Perhaps you are wondering how we dare to bring in women from the outside world on such occasions as this. No doubt you share the misconception of so many others that we monastics resort to the women of our convents for such purposes. That is entirely false. What may have been in the earlier days of the church is of course beyond our knowledge and control; but in all sincerity I can assure you that we laborers in the Lord's vineyard value too highly the soul that is dedicated to Christ to dare lead it astray. The Lord in His boundless grace can well forgive the sins of you women who have never been His, who have never seen the Light. But of those already pledged to Him, He is majestically jealous. We have more than enough as it is to prevent immorality in the convents—much less do we consider launching them upon the paths of sensuality. And so, whenever the need forces us, and I fear that the very nature of our work, by its peculiar necessity of repression, makes it all too frequent, we call upon women of the more worldly kind, and thus despoil Heaven of no soul.

"As to possible reflections upon the clergy, we have no fear. So deeply entrenched is the universal respect of our power and integrity, that if you were ever to recount the events of this night to all the world, none would believe you anything but mad.

"Does it follow then that we vicars of the Lord are walking in the ways of hypocrisy? No, my daughter. It is merely that we have been compelled to adopt a deep sense of expediency in addition to our sense of duty. As shepherds of the people, we have an important task to fulfill. Marriage and the family— these are the institutions that are absolutely essential to the stability of society and its perpetuation; hence we must foster them. But yet, as Plato has pointed out, the narrowness of these same institutions, their self-seeking, is inconsistent with the idea of broader social service, such as that of the church. If we were to have wives and children, our first concern would in the nature of things be for them and not for the millions that we must lead. That we forego these is at once the proof of our sincerity and our altruism. Hence arises the concept of celibacy for the clergy, and we do all in our power to follow it by living simply and thinking purely. But while all of us may be spiritually fitted to our task, yet there are many of us who physically are still attached to the earth—and this is a thing beyond our personal dispensation; it is in the hands of the Lord. If we must satisfy our flesh, then in all humility we must. And since to do so openly would countenance a profligacy in the people that would soon destroy society, since to admit our weakness would deprive us of that prestige which is necessary—not for our own good, mind you, but for the welfare of mankind—we deem such expedients as these the best compromise between our heavenly and our earthly heritage."

As he concluded, my gaze leapt to the varied tableaux being staged all about us. What a maze of heaving joy-contorted loins and feverish thighs! And Manon, finished her first fuck while I sat talking, and having started on her second, with a lechery that I had never dreamt she possessed, was shouting at the top of her voice "Come on, you stiff-pricked stags! Come on, I'll fuck you all! Come on! I'll take everyone of you on at once!" And surely enough, as those heretofore nonparticipating eagerly approached, she received one in the delicious enclosure of her cunt, another in the not less delightful haven of her pretty luscious mouth, and still two others she accommodated by manipulating their impatient scarlet cocks in each of her soft, well-groomed hands, while all her many lovers in turn squabbled for possession of her pert firm breasts. It was more than I could stand in continued inactivity.

"Pardon me, Father," I said with some embarrassment, "I feel deeply honored at your deeming me worthy of your words—and

I shall not soon forget them. But would you mind if I jumped in just for a little while? Don't you see how unfair it is to my little Manon for me to sit idly here while she is being torn to bits by four of your voracious pontiffs?"

"Go, of course, my daughter, with my blessings," he replied kindly, and drawing a little volume of sacred meditations from his sleeve he settled back to fortify himself against what must have been for him a very wearisome situation indeed.

And now—to the rescue—true to rescue form, discarding my clothes as I went. I was nearly too late, for Manon's mollient, dextrous fingers were just bringing on the supreme surrender of the man to her right, who, just as I approached, yielded up his creamy tribute in thick copious jets, every drop of which spelled for me pleasures that I had been missing. And the two who occupied her lower and upper mouths respectively, excited by the sight of this triumph, joined him in ejaculation almost immediately after, flooding both of her warm caressing orifices with their prolific love-juices simultaneously, even ere the last spurt had shot from the turgid gland of the first, past her supple milking hand and onto her wildly heaving bosom. Only the remaining gentleman, whether due to the weaker manipulative power of her left hand or to greater staying qualities of his own, still withheld his final offering. I slipped alongside him and gently released his bursting crimson bone from her soft perspiring grasp. Manon, trembling in the throes of her own dizzy climax, with eyes tensely shut, and inundated with these triple sacrifices, scarcely noticed the deprivation of a fourth, but continued wildly pumping both her hands, working her transfixed cunt in mad jerks, and sucking away for dear life at the spouting prick that filled her mouth.

Leading the cock that I had captured to a nearby heap of cushions, without so much as glancing at the face of its owner, I threw myself on my back and stuffed it into my swimming cunt, praying only that it would not go off too soon, imploring only that it would not lose its stiff stamina before I should catch up with it.

"Fuck me!" I panted. I was consumed with lechery . . . and lest my rider should fail to understand me, I inaugurated the essential movements by my own initiative. The hungry lips of my feverish cunt ran up and down the solid morsel of flesh that distended me, as if seeking a point at which it might bite it off satisfactorily without getting too little and at the same time finding that all was too much for it.

Such greedy maneuvering soon had the expected result. Before my partner could even well adopt the intricate rhythm of my lustful abandoned motions, we both came off together in a climax of nerve-dazzling splendor. But men who live in the monasteries, as I had learned before, are a single round of love's soft ammunition. Without pausing to reload or even to allow the breech to cool, he continued pounding away. Ram for ram I responded, and when the next tally was taken, I was one ahead of him—though completely exhausted. Only then did we rest for a moment, his organ still stiff and soaking in my seething cunt. He introduced himself.

"I'm not even a cardinal," he said, "just secretary to one of the archbishops. That's why I was the last to be taken care of. But if I am the last to get started—and by the Madonna I've scarcely begun—I'll be the last to finish. Ready for another yet?"

I wanted a few more moments of respite; but he was raring to go. So I varied the routine a bit, first washing his blood-gorged dripping member with some fresh champagne, drying it with a napkin, and then giving him my best in the French manner.

When he had finished filling my mouth with the proofs of his still unabated potency, he immediately demanded another.

"What a man!" I exclaimed, "but I'm not going to let you be so selfish this time. Do you know the sixty-nine?"

"Yes," he responded, "though I've never tried it."

"Well, there's no time like the present to start learning. If you don't object to doing it—after your coming in me—"

"Why should I?" he put in unhesitantly. "It's my own, isn't it? If you can stand it, I suppose I can. Let's get started."

And we did—I above him to restrain him from shoving his still menacing member too far down my throat, he with his head smothered between my thighs as I crouched over him in the ingenious reversed position. That he liked it was evidenced by the quickness with which he learned his part and the passionate eagerness with which he drew my buttocks down toward him and crushed his face into my cunt as I gave down spending after spending of pleasure into his avid mouth.

At this stage we declared time out and paused for some refreshments. While my partner was getting me a glass of wine, a slightly tipsy bishop with a flushed eager mien rushed me and took hold of me.

"Why, here's one I haven't screwed yet!" he exclaimed. "Down you must go, mam'zelle. I'm passing nothing up tonight. For who knows when I'll get another woman? Do you take it *a la garcon-cul?*"

I was anxious to please. But still—"Do you have any pomade? Vaseline? Cold cream?" I queried, regarding his huge member a bit doubtfully. "The path you choose to follow has no lubrications of its own, as I suppose you know well enough." He laughed heartily at my innuendo, and reaching over to a sideboard where there was an array of fancy foods, he with his fingers flicked some whipped cream off the top of a pastry.

"This will do in a pinch, my daughter," he said as he spread it over the expansive head of his crimson cock.

"Why that looks good enough to eat," I sallied.

"Oh, you French girls!" the bishop guffawed, "always looking for something to eat. But that's against the laws of nature. So we're going to do it *per viam rectum*," and then he stopped to laugh at his rather obvious Latin pun.

But the first sight of my shapely, jutting posterior as I leaned over a chair expectantly soon put my ecclesiastic in a more serious frame of mind. I felt the bulging badge of his manhood pry asunder the two firm hemispheres of my buttocks and—suffice it that whipped cream *will* do in a pinch, dear reader, and suffice it that my man did his work with the easy skill of an old pilot seasoned to back channels and thoroughly acquainted with the navigation of the narrow and illicit but nonetheless delicious rear canal.

Other couples, noting our happy example, soon followed suit.

"Why this feels just like home!" shouted one of the less discreet cardinals, as with arms wrapped about Yvette's soft naked waist he drove fiercely up into her tight rosy rear enclosure. And two of the "stags," having no women, for lack of better and released from their final restraint, uncovered themselves and proceeded forthwith to commit the detestable crime of buggery, the one of them forcing his prick up into that passage of the other which is alas common to both sexes. Lightly as we might talk of such vice when far removed from it, to be confronted with its actual perpetration so shamelessly was enough to revolt the senses.

The old man on the platform, glancing up from the perusal of his livery, and for the first time noting what went on, arose in indignation.

"Gentleman!" he cried, "we have been lenient enough with you, we think. But we cannot countenance this vile re-creation of the sinful city of Sodom—and before our very eyes! We are leaving your gathering at once and wish to have it understood that we strongly decry and disapprove of your conduct." An attendant rushed to his aid and he left the room.

"That means we all have to do penance with an extra mass tomorrow," my partner confided to me, "but it's worth it!" he went on, as he resumed a vigorous movement that soon flooded my bowels with a generous load of his boiling sperm.

"And now, my dear mademoiselle," my bishop remarked as soon as he had recovered enough of his breath to speak, "you are in too well-oiled a condition to even consider withdrawing. May I continue?"

I was beginning to feel a bit tired; many of the others were dropping out of the lists too, what with the exhaustion of love and the final triumph of wine. But I kept my posterior arched and let him go on. By the time the last drop of his juice had been pumped up from his capacious reservoirs as they swung back and forth against my tightly distended anus, and had been catapulted into my entrails by his powerful male duct, everyone had called quits except for ourselves and one other couple.

My rider, vanquished at last, retrieved his spent arrow and we went over to watch the sole survivors of this long amorous marathon. They were, as the reader may have guessed, Manon, who had got it first and wanted it still, and the slighted secretary who had given me four rounds of his shot and Lord knows how many to others since then. He was still at it, pounding away—in the proper spot, I might add—as if it were his first. Manon was returning tit for tat with a vengeance, but oh what a flushed and bedraggled sight she was—her hair wildly dishevelled, her palpitating bubbies bruised from much handling, her shapely thighs streaked with perspiration and spend. She was moaning and moving about uneasily as her "nth" pleasurable climax approached, her milk-white belly heaving, her feverish buttocks writhing passionately as she pressed up to meet the impact of her assailant. How he was giving it to her! Fatigued as I was, I felt my pulses awakening with envious desire.

"Enough!" panted Manon, when, having poured down her maiden joy-flow, he still continued his mad prodding.

"No, no! Another! I'm not finished yet! groaned her vanquisher as she squirmed to get out from under his relentless drill. He fucked her all the more vigorously and determinedly. Manon emitted a pitiful quavering scream as his bar brushed her sensitive insides anew. That cry pierced to my heart.

"Man! man!" I expostulated, seizing the assaulter by the shoulder, "haven't you enough decency to leave off when the lady says she can't stand anymore? Do you want to make her hysterical?"

"Well," protested the insatiable fuckster as he withdrew two-thirds of his scarlet probe from the soaking, rosy depths of her twitching swollen snatch, "what am I to do with this stubborn unsatisfied beast? If I stop halfway while it's so stiff, it won't go down in weeks!"

"All right, then," I replied half-reluctantly, "let up on my little Manon and I'll let you stable it with me."

He made the transfer with alacrity, and I

his fresher steed, enlivened by my short rest and the vision of his earlier performances, leaped and twisted under him to give him the maximum of action in the minimum of time. And though I had scarcely expected it, I twice gave down a discharge of womanly bliss before his soft substance had shot from him to soothe my irritated membranes.

But heavens! The satyr was still stiff—and demanded yet another encounter. I pushed him from me in despair, turning a deaf ear to his pleadings. Two of my other girls, however, had come up to watch this male marvel's last bout—all the others had fallen asleep in various undignified postures about the room—and they agreed to take him in hand.

"Remember your own advice, Mademoiselle Madeleine," Giselle said to me laughingly as she proceeded to give his unbending member its second champagne bath of the evening prior to taking it in her mouth, "there's nothing like a fully satisfied customer." And while Yvette furnished some auxiliary titillations, putting one of her soft chubby breasts in the subject's mouth, Giselle went down on him in a fashion to make me proud of her, and calculated to soon deprive this hard customer of his obstinacy. If any of my male readers happen to doubt the possibility of this man's virility as I picture it, I can only suggest that he live celebately in a monastery for a few months and then set to with as attractive a group of girls as my company presented.

Considerably exhausted by now, I drew up an armchair to sit and watch—drying my dripping vagina with a soft silk handkerchief that I had held clenched in my fist through thick and thin. For all the exquisite treatment he was receiving at their hands and lips, our "last stand" was a long time in finishing. The show was becoming monotonous. I grew sleepy. In the candelabra the candles were fluttering and flicking and going out altogether. Beside the soft liquid sound of Giselle's practiced lips, nothing could be heard but the snores of these combatants long since vanquished.

I must have dozed off for a time, for when I opened my eyes next, it was Yvette who was tonguing that troublesome shaft, while Giselle stood by nursing her aching jaws.

"How is it coming, dearie?" I asked her.

"Oh, we're on a second now," she replied "but we expect to reach bottom soon. There wasn't but a drop or two that came out last time."

Even as we discussed the problem, the conclusion drew nigh. Our gentleman, stiffening with the approach of his terrific pleasure, was plunging his part desperately in and out of Yvette's lovely mouth, his hand fiercely straining her head to him as he wrapped his fingers in the silken strands of her beautiful blonde hair. Suddenly, with a sharp cry, half of ecstasy and half of anguish, he pushed her violently away from him. A tiny spurt of creamy white shot from his enspasmed urethra, and in its wake a few drops of fresh scarlet blood. We had indeed drained him. The stubborn tool now at last dropped its head and retired, completely beaten, while it's owner fell into a fitful exhausted slumber.

The three of us who alone remained awake,

surveyed the battlefield triumphantly. **While** everyone lay with his intimate nudity fully exposed, the reader may accept my assurance that there wasn't a cock left standing. Our job was done, and gloriously well done. A decided chillness in the air told us it would soon be morning. Gently we awakened Manon and Henriette, retrieved our scattered clothes and dressed ourselves hurriedly. Shaking up our reluctant, sleepy conductor, Monsignor X., we set him aright and left the orgy behind us just as the first rays of a cold dawn broke through the curtained windows and just as the bells of Saint Peter's nearby began ringing out their resonant call to early mass.

"Must we stop at this dump hotel another day?" complained Manon when we got back to our forbidding *albergo*. "I wish I were back in Paris, snoozing right now in my nice broad bed."

"There is a train deluxe with sleepers that leaves for Paris at 7:20—in exactly one hour," suggested the monsignor. "You could just make it."

"We will!" shouted the girls in unison. "Who wants to hang around this fearful graveyard? Home and Paris it is!"

I gave my consent, although I myself was still determined to remain in Rome a few days longer to do some sightseeing. While our host hurried ahead to reserve places on the express, we packed our belongings and then followed to the station. I saw my girls off, each of them kissing me dutifully, and then with Monsignor X took a taxi to transfer to some more luxurious hotel.

In the cab my partner raised an unexpected complaint.

"I was so busy seeing to things," he said, "that I scarcely had a chance to get anything for myself. No more than two—or three at most. Look—just feel that hard-on if you don't believe me."

I apologized for not removing my glove and felt of his proffered tool. Surely enough, it was as hard as iron. I breathed a sigh of resignation.

"All right, Monsignor," I assented, "I'll let you come to bed with me at the hotel. But do remember that I'm terribly tired and do need some sleep."

And so it goes, dear reader. Our work is never done. Like the warriors that sprang up again and again when Cadmus sowed the dragon's teeth, so for every erection we conquer, another—or perhaps two or three—rise up in its stead to beset our pleasant but arduous path.

# CHAPTER ELEVEN

A day or two later in my peregrinations about the Eternal City, I took a *carozza* and rode out to the suburbs to examine the famed Baths of Caracalla. It being a weekday, the neighborhood was entirely deserted, except for a rather handsome young Italian guide of olive hue who approached and offered to show me through the ruins and explain them in any one of four or five languages—none of which he spoke very well. I accepted his services—and thanks to his information, I for the first time learned the real former character of the place. It had been nothing less than a colossal house of pleasure —with numerous finely tiled bathing pools and steam rooms, true, but also with scores of private cubicles and larger orgy chambers in which were satisfied those needs naturally aroused in the course of bathing.

It really was a stupendous affair. And as I wandered through the roofless ruined pleasure rooms, I seemed to feel in the warm silent atmosphere ghostly vibrations of the magnificent lusts of the hot-blooded Romans that burned themselves out between these still standing walls. For instance, what a cozy little nook there . . . only, instead of the yellow silken robes of Pamphilia or of Hostia strewn about as they are stripped by the impatient hands of the desirous Propertius, there are yellowing sheets of discarded newspapers, refuse—and yes, as evidence that though Propertius and Hostia and Pamphilia are long dead, desire still lives on, there are numerous used condoms strewn around, and there a torn soiled handkerchief, stained with the virgin blood of some 20th century Italian miss.

I have read somewhere a theory to the effect that women, in the face of death or destruction, become especially lustful, insofar as their reproductive instinct is called upon by nature to repopulate and repair the loss. Since I do not acknowledge the existence of any such thing as the reproductive instinct—since the mere desire for sexual pleasure explains matters much more satisfactorily to me—I cannot subscribe to the theory. Yet it does indicate how I might have been affected by these desolate surroundings, if not by the actual memory of glorious rites, both ancient and recent, that had been celebrated here. The hot Italian sun was no inconsiderable factor too, in arousing my blood and my fancies.

I stepped up onto a fragment of a broken marble cornice—ostensibly to get a better view around me—but actually to give my swarthy, handsome guide a glimpse of my legs and figure and test his reaction to them. A smoldering glint came into his eyes. The Latin temperament is indeed easily ignited. It soon became obvious that at the slightest further provocation he would rape me.

A soft warm wind played about my dress, molding the thin diaphanous material to the voluptuous contours of my body. I bent over to tighten my shoestrings. Without actually raising my dress, I pulled up my silk stockings, snapping my garter with a luscious "smack" as I did so. My companion took a threatening step closer, his eyes narrowing, his face flushing hotly. Blithely reaching him my hand, I jumped off my low pedestal, landing close up to his tensed body and looking smilingly into his face.

A struggle seemed to be going on within him. He was obviously at a loss to interpret my foreign ways of coquettishness. I settled his mind by boldly leading his hand to my bosom. His countenance lighted up joyfully as he pressed my bubbies for a moment, then, immediately after, he returned the compliment by leading my hand to a part of his own anatomy that resembled flesh far less than bone. My soft caressing hand, encompassing the goodly bulk of its circumference with difficulty, once or twice gently peeled back the foreskin from the dull crimson head. That object, in this moment of my soft, rich desire, represented to me not merely the symbol, but the very essence, the veritable godhead of maleness.

I would have enjoyed holding on to that firm, reassuring, velvety limb of flesh awhile longer; but my companion, with a perhaps excusable impatience, wrenched it from my grasp and proceeded to force me to the ground.

"*Nolete, mio amice!*" I whispered. "Don't! The ground is dirty. We can do it standing —this way."

And as his urgent hands ran down my body, I helped him raise my dress up above my waist, where I held it from slipping with my chin. As late May in southern Italy is as hot as Paris in midsummer, I of course had on no underthings to impede him further. Thus uncovered, my rich silky brown pubic triangle made a most pleasing contrast in the bright sun against the dazzling white of my belly and of my shapely thighs—now still close-meeting but in a moment to kiss each other adieu to make way for the lovely intruder. Still holding up my skirts, I raised my right leg sideways and rested it on a convenient block of stone. My cunt was thus brought forward and my legs held apart as effectively as if I were on my back with a well-stuffed cushion beneath my posteriors.

My partner caught the idea immediately. Bracing me with one of his hands behind my soft buttocks, he bent his knees a trifle, and bringing the point of his fine instrument up between the gaping lips of my expectant cunny, he sent the thing up and home to the hilt with a single motion as sudden and impetuous as the thrust of a stilletto. I winced with pain and delight as the broad bulldog-like head forcibly clove asunder the adhering membranes to the maximum and came up full against the cul-de-sac of my cunt. It seemed as if my whole body and being were upheld by the length and strength and thickness of the firm shaft that impaled me.

My Italian, too hot-blooded by nature to brook much dallying, now with both his hands on my posteriors, was withdrawing part way to shove home once more. I joined him with an oscillating spiral motion of my cunt that was especially facilitated by my unimpeded standing position.

It was superb! The full horizontal strokes that his bar bestowed upon my clitty were all that I could possibly have wished. Only, indeed, as the taller waves of sensation began washing over me and I grew faint with pleasure, it required a decided effort to keep my feet when all my impulses now were to sink to the ground. His wand continued working its magic, running up and down the tight torrid length of my clasping sheath. My skirts still furled up onto my heaving bosom, my bare belly palpitating with excitement and with the reflex action of my pumping cunny, I continued madly gyrating my middle upon the firm axis that he furnished. I took a last glance downwards; through a hot misty maze I could see his proud penis plunging rapidly in and out of the glistening box beneath my brown pubic thatch. Then my head fell back as I abondoned myself to the quick overpowering augmentation of sensation that his operations were affording me.

*"Viene?* (Are you coming?)" my partner soon gasped to me, betraying by his uncontrolled breathing that he too was approaching the final extremity.

*"Vengo . . . preset . . . Mi aspetti!* (I am coming—soon. Wait for me!)" I managed to reply falteringly.

*"Allora pronto!* (Then be quick!)" he groaned brokenly, clutching wildly at the soft flesh of my buttocks. Desperately, my body all atremble, I fucked back for the life of me—in short tense jabs that gave my clitty hell. At last! I felt it coming!

"Now!" I veritably screamed, forgetting myself, and speaking not Italian and not French but my native English: "Now! Give it to me! Oh, you dear damned garlic-eater! Give it to me!"

He did. Two or three vicious, bone-breaking shoves were my reward, our bodies tensed, and just as I reached the dizzy climax of bliss, I felt spouting up within the seething crater of my cunt, the thick burning lava of his own enjoyment. My head lay on his shoulder as we both continued fitfully moving. The explosion of delicious sensation within me, unbearable in its intensity, had me sobbing and moaning and beating my partner with my fists and crying, "Oh, oh! Wop, you fucking bastard, I love you!"

Even as the good feeling ended, my turbulent center continued twitching spasmodically back and forth, to make our paradise last as long as possible. Only the common necessity to sit down or lean on something compelled our separation. The huge flesh bolt that had worked such turmoil in my senses slipped from me with a moist, audible "cluck." Immediately, the quantity of our mutual spendings, released by this sudden unplugging of my cunt, gushed out and began dribbling down the soft inner sides of my thighs toward the tops of my silk stockings. With my frail gossamer handkerchief I tried to staunch the flow; but of course its capacity of absorption was far too limited to avail me much, and in a moment it was soaked beyond all usefulness. My partner, however, noting my predicament, with native gallantry whipped his brightly colored bandanna from about his neck, and after wiping his own dripping part, passed it to me with a polite bow. Tossing my own away and thus adding it to the other similar souvenirs of the ages that I have mentioned, I mopped up the rest of the sticky fluid and handed him back his handkerchief. He shook it out carefully and hung it on a stone ledge in the sun to dry, explaining that he would get it on his next trip.

Straightening my clothes as well as I could, we continued our inspection of the ruins; but now so half-heartedly that soon I decided to give it up. Anyway, it was quite obvious that my guide wanted to talk cunt and not history, while I as a matter of fact was so exhausted by my unusually straining fuck that I wasn't much in the mood to appreciate either subject.

"Perhaps I hurt you, signorina?" he asked with timid solicitude when he noticed my apparent distraction. "Was I too big for you?"

"Oh no, my dear man," I reassured him, "I like them big. In fact, the bigger the better."

"Ah! Then the signorina should meet my friend Luigi. He is gifted with an equipment alongside of which mine is as nothing!"

"Indeed?" I put in, somewhat infected by his enthusiasm.

"Ah, yes! And how all the girls are crazy about him! He takes them all away from me."

"Really? I should like to meet your marvelous friend."

"If the signorina will but leave her address and say when she will be disposed. . ."

I wrote out for him the name of the hotel at which I was stopping and suggested 2 o'clock the next afternoon as a convenient hour. His friend, like most Italians apparently, managed to live without working.

As we parted at the entrance to the ruins, a huge Cook's sightseeing bus drove up, crowded with rubbering robots from my own native land—America. I paused to watch the queer chattering cargo. One of their number, a rather prim-looking young lady of about 25 whom I sized up at once as a schoolteacher, wearing clothes of a decidedly masculine cut, seemed especially familiar to me. She too was looking at me rather intently. As the passengers filed off the bus, I suddenly recognized her. It was my old classmate, Sylvia Watson, she of the dubious high-school-lavatory incident over eight years ago. Putting two and two together, there was no mistaking the line of development that *she* had followed. I approached her. She too recognized and greeted me; but there was a snooty constraint about her manner, a sort of sneery condescension and leering curiosity that cut me deeply. I thought of the circumstances under which I had left home, the impression that must have been made on my narrow-minded Plattsburg friends. I couldn't let the matter rest thus. Sylvia was to me the representative of that past. I wanted to justify myself in her eyes. Or failing that, I wished to wipe out her detestable air of superiority by telling her just how thoroughly I saw through her soured homosexuality.

I invited her to visit me at my hotel.

"Oh, I don't know, Louise. I'm so busy. There are so many things to see here in Rome. Tomorrow we're going to the Diocletan, and the day after . . . but I would like to hear what you've been doing all these years . . . Maybe I *will* get a chance to drop in on you."

"Yes, do, Sylvia," I replied in the hypocritical saccharine manner which women find so necessary in their social intercourse; but which, thank God, I was generally able to get along without. In truth, I would have liked to scratch her eyes out.

"But if I do come," the creature smirked, "there won't be any men with you, will there?"

I reassured her, intimating even for my purpose—though she seemed skeptical—that I too disliked the male sex and was a sympathizer with the "great sisterhood" of which she was no doubt a member. She left me to rejoin her party while I took a *fiacre* and returned to my hotel for a much-needed bath.

# CHAPTER TWELVE

Next afternoon, at 2 o'clock sharp, the desk clerk sent up to my suite to notify me that two rough looking natives were asking for me. I explained that they were to do some work for me on a villa that I had just purchased and asked that they be ushered up.

My friend Benito of the day before entered, dragging behind him a great hulking companion whom he introduced as Luigi. Both of them were crudely but neatly dressed, and their skins shone with perhaps unaccustomed ablutions.

I offered them some wine and tried to make them feel more at ease by striking up a conversation; but it soon became apparent that both of them were hopelessly uneducated and stupid, and Benito's glib explanation of the Baths the day proceeding had no doubt been a memorized spiel, delivered parrotlike. I felt a little ashamed of myself for having made an engagement with such lowly characters; but there was no thought in my mind of disappointing them when they had taken such pains to prepare for the occasion.

Leading them to my boudoir, which they entered with awe, hats in hand, as if visiting a cathedral, I drew the blinds to shut out the glare of the sun and got right down to business.

"Where is this marvelous equipment you told me of yesterday, Benito?" I asked. He addressed his friend in some, to me, incomprehensible dialect. Luigi seemed to be protesting, but finally, at his companion's insistence, nervously unbuttoned his trousers and brought out the subject of our discussion. Unexpected as had been the order to "present arms," and extinguished as was the simple-minded Italian by the luxury of his surroundings, yet his semistiff organ was of a size and bulk to make me burningly curious to see it at its best. With my soft tapering fingers I laid hold of the bent sword. Under my cunning caresses it took but a moment to make the yard as straight and august as any I had ever handled. Luigi nearly fainted with embarrassment at my unexpectedly direct procedure, but a grateful grin illuminated his features as he stood, awkward and submissively awaiting the end of my inspection. Lowering his trousers to see the rest of his attributes, I weighed on the palm of my hand his heavy bag of love's elixir, estimating in my mind how many cuntfuls its spacious chambers could afford me.

Satisfied with my investigation, and my further interest aroused, I added at least another inch each way to the size of his member by slowly and provocatively removing, first my dressing gown, then each of my silk stockings, and lastly my alluring crepe chemise. I then had both Luigi and Benito strip to the skin— and let me record that, relieved of their cheap vulgar clothing they were a pair of bronze heroes out of some classic Greek frieze—with this one important qualification: while the ancient sculptors presented their male figures with insignificant flaccid sex parts such as would cast doubt on the gender of even a child, these two before me had their forms completed by a pair of bars eligible for consideration as major limbs of the human body.

Climbing up on my sumptuous double bed, allowing my well-rounded buttocks to jut out maddeningly, I called to Luigi to follow. He held back.

"What is it?" I inquired impatiently.

"*E troppo bello*," he stammered, pointing to the silk and lace counterpanes. The bed was too luxurious for the simple-hearted Italian to dare muss it. I suppose he wanted to do it on the floor. But we compromised thusly. Seating him in a comfortable chair, I mounted his lap facing him. As much to get my own lubrications working prior to undertaking the invagination of his monstrous cock as to make him lose all self-consciousness, I coaxed a stiff-nippled tit between his lips and, wrapping my legs tightly about his brawny waist, held him in the tender clutch of my soft white thighs while I rubbed my silky mount up and down his belly and chest, till the lips of my cunt became tingly and moist.

Soon he caught the spirit of the thing; but it was only when the upstanding stiffness of his organ became such as to threaten crashing through me at one point if not at another that I decided to let it in where it belonged. What a rich and randy delight as I sat down slowly upon the erect shaft, letting it feed into me with exquisite deliberateness! The usually oval shape of my cunt was for once, I could plainly see, stretched into a distended O-shape by the bulk and circumference of the welcomed intruder. So my plump dewy nether lips were clinging to the very root of it, our pubic bushes interwoven, while at the other end the swollen head battered against the mouth of my avid womb.

Thus deliciously skewered upon his prodder, I contented myself with minor wrigglings for a while—to give my muscles and glands a chance to adapt themselves to the truncheon distender and better oil the now open road to voluptuousness. Then—slowly at first and then more rapidly—I began the full oscillation of my agile buttocks, giving the utmost play to my throbbing, quivering cunt, and rubbing the hard slippery little lump of flesh that is my clitty against the broad velvety bulk of his prick. That magical little touchstone soon had me weltering in enjoyment. My soft clinging sheath was yielding up its secretions so generously that I could feel the soft mucous dribbling down over the root of his prick and balls. Slow, long thrusts and short digs succeeded each other in turn. Sometimes we would pause for a moment to leisurely savor the close carnal conjunction of our bodies. My partner, competent as he might have been no doubt, had but little left to do that I did not take care of in his stead. Just as we were about to settle down to the steady concupiscent canter that would carry us to our goal, however, Benito, who had been till now standing by watching us jealously, his rod held sheepishly in his hands, approached and demanded some part in the activities. Impatient, to avoid delay, I took his prick in my mouth while he stood in front of me behind the chair on which Luigi and I were engaged. Only a little hampered by this second prick to take care of and the necessity to keep it between my lips despite all the jolting I should give and receive, we resumed our delicious game of peg in the hole after only a nominal interruption.

With the approach of the final celestial rapture, my bounds became so frantic as to have unseated me, had not Luigi's rampant weapon held me well transfixed. What vigorous writhings and oscillating motions ensued, as, urged on by the tormenting pleasure, we separated our feverish mounts only to shove them together again with mad violence. My partner's hands were still holding onto my buttocks, pressing and pulling on them, handling the plump cheeks like a pair of cymbals, tightening and relaxing the stricture of my cunt upon his cock by this outside pressure. By inserting one of his fingers into my anus—which was now twitching spasmodically in unison with my cunny—he bestowed upon me an even further bawdy, lustful joy . . . .

All this time I sucked faithfully and desperately on Benito's by-no-means negligible penis —to keep him apace with us if possible. But now, with the uncontrollable floods of sensation gathering in me, with cords of fiery pleasure knotting all my fibers, I found it increasingly difficult to coordinate the sucking action of my lips and tongue with the necessary movements of my lips, loins and cunt. Blindly, feverishly, uttering spasmodic sobs and stifled cries, I took the to me superfluous and distracting roll of flesh in my hand, removed it from my mouth and pushed it far away from me. Then, burying my burning face in Luigi's shoulder and wrapping my legs more tightly about his back, I gave myself up entirely and selfishly to the attainment of the delicious end.

A few more wild tense movements of my

hips—dictated by some deep impulse within me, rather than by any conscious volition of my own—and as his large soul-satisfying staff of life glided quickly up and down my quivering channel, the ultimate acme of bliss burst upon me in veritable sheets of flame. My salacious cunt took one last sweep around his engine with a tense spiral motion, then my whole body stiffened with convulsive rigidity as a long low wail of rapture was torn from me. Luigi, gasping explosively, himself intercepted at the very apex of pleasure, and finding my up-to-now active cunt suddenly paralyzed, raised my body with his hands till his bursting prick had retreated to the very mouth of my cunt, then with a single crushing motion rammed it back into me to the hilt. A moment later he poured into my lust-maddened body his burning priceless treasure of liquified pearl. My twitching cunt muscles would not release him until, in their sweet agony, they had pressed the last drop of that soothing spermatic joy from him—then I collapsed in a soft breathless hysteria of relief.

Even before I could entirely recover myself, Benito was at my side demanding his turn. I was not a bit averse to more of the erect yard's steady application, but I did want a breathing spell. Just then there was a knock at the door. Climbing quickly off Luigi's lap, and slipping into a kimono, I hastened to answer it, with the effusions of my encounter still trickling down my thighs. It was the hotel boy, to tell me that there was a Signorina Watson below to see me.

"Send her up," I said. On the instant a malicious idea had come to me. Hastening back to my male guests, I explained that I was to have a visitor, bundled them into the bathroom with their clothes and an album of erotic photographs that I had recently wheedled from one of the cardinals, to keep them in form, and then locked the door on them until I should have further need of their services. I dried my cunny superficially and went to admit Sylvia.

"Oh, what a beautiful room you have here, Louise!" was her first exclamation as she entered.

"There are two more to the suite, my dear Sylvia," I made sure to add.

"But how can you afford such expensive accommodations? Where do you get the money?"

"Oh, I've held various positions. And I still work hard on occasion. But tell me about yourself—about the folks at home."

We chatted for a while, sitting close together. The way she had of putting her hands on my thighs as she spoke, while certainly permissible between members of the same sex, further confirmed my suspicions about her tastes. I played it up further by allowing my peignoir to droop open, letting her see one of my ripe luscious breasts entirely bare. Her eyes glistened.

"What a gorgeous kimono you have, Louise," she said stiltedly, reaching over to feel the material, and incidentally brushing my soft flesh.

"Yes, I'll tell you where you can buy one just like it. Look how well-made it is. Look at this hand embroidered hem and the satin lining on the inside," and deliberately, I raised the whole lower part of the gown, uncovering my bare thighs up to my dark *accent circonflex*. Her face flushed exitedly. She was really quit pretty, I had to admit against my will, except for the ridiculous masculine costume that she affected, and for a certain virgin primness about her that struck me disagreeably.

Allowing my gown to sag open more, I took her hand in mine, resting it in my warm, bare lap, and spoke confidentially:

"Do you remember that afternoon in the school lavatory, Sylvia, when I caught you and Miriam Smith together? I have often wondered what you two were doing to each other. Come, tell me. I'll understand."

"Well," Sylvia spoke in a hoarse low tone, "we had been fingering each other."

"Is that all?"

"There was more—but we didn't know about it at that time." As she spoke, I could feel her fingers burrowing gently between my close-meeting thighs, trying to gain access to my cunt. I kept my legs close together—and she could proceed no further. There was a long silence.

"Let's play with each other, Louise," she finally managed to utter in a prurient broken whisper. I made no reply.

"You don't like me?" she asked pathetically.

"Not in those horrible clothes you are wearing."

"I'll take them off."

"All right—and then we shall see."

Anxious to please me, Sylvia sprang to her feet and removed her hat and coat, and then her skirt. She was still fully covered with underthings of plain white linen, spotlessly clean indeed, but in the most god-awful taste. I helped her undo the string of her petticoat; she pulled it down and stepped out of it. Now I could discern that her legs were quite passable, with fine shapely calves. Hesitant and blushing, she pulled up her linen chemise and slipped it off over her head. A bare, dimpled belly came into view, and then a pair of dainty little breasts, each tipped with a tiny scarlet rose. With the removal of each article of her ugly clothing, she was becoming more and more attractive. As I aided her in pulling down her bloomers, baring the spare but shapely columns of her thighs and the undulation of her neat posteriors, I could see that she was in fact quite beautiful—in every sense of the word meant for good honest fucking, but by some misarrangement of circumstances curbing her charms and saving them for the barren embraces of other females.

Seating herself for a moment and crossing her legs to remove her stocking, with the ankle of one leg over the knee of the other, I could see at the juncture of her thighs her rosy garden of delight, bowered in thick dusky foliage and differing from any other adorable cunt only in that it had probably never been pilfered by man, and that the little elflike clitty that dwells therein and is usually out of sight was in her case a bit overdeveloped by handling or suction, and was peeping insolently out from between the plump pink casements of its delightful palace.

I led her into the bedroom and insisted on her trying on one my flimsy silk combinations that had nothing but a frail ribbon across the crotch.

"Don't you like yourself much better this way?" I asked. She was indeed indisputably alluring now.

"Oh, I don't know—" she said, throwing her arms about me, "it makes me feel so—so frivilous. Let me take it off." I did not insist.

She joined me on the bed, where I allowed her to caress me as she would. First timidly, then more boldly, her hands made the whole circuit of my body. Soon her lips followed. On my own part, I acted noncommittally. As she reached my cunt with her lips, she looked up and said.

"Let's do it together, Louise. It's not fair that I should do it for you and you not for me."

"I don't like it that way, Sylvia," I lied. "I like to concentrate on what I'm doing, whether it's enjoying the thrill myself or making some-one else enjoy it. Anyway, you can't do it so well with the thing upside down. Your tongue doesn't go in so far. You do it first, then I will."

"But if I do it first, you may not want to do it for me after," she objected shrewdly. "You lick mine first."

"It works either way, Sylvia. But you started it, I didn't. Either take it or leave it. It's all the same to me," and I pretended to be leaving the bed. She held me back.

"All right," she grumbled, "spread your legs; but Louise, if you refuse to lick mine later, I'll never speak to you again."

I would have liked to wring the little vixen's neck; but I had my own plans. What a shame, I thought, that such a delicious piece should possess so detestable a temperament, so small a character. Perhaps, I myself might have become that way too if I had remained in Plattsburg's cramping atmosphere all my life.

With none of the passion or impetuousness that might have excused the act, but with only a venal surreptitiousness that seemed to proclaim, "I know I oughtn't be doing this, I know it's wrong; but you won't tell on me," she started tonguing my cunt. The unaccustomed moistness and creamy content that had so recently been injected into that part made her pause.

"I'd hate to think, Louise," she spoke liquidly from between my things, "that I was putting my mouth where a man had just been."

"Don't be a fool, Sylvia," I said impatiently, "do you think I'd be satisfied with your awkward little tongue if I could have a big stiff dolly in me right now?"

"Louise!" she exclaimed sharply, "how can you talk that way to me? I won't do another thing for you!"

"Little hypocrite!" I retorted. "Do you mean that you've never longed to have a man's long velvety thing sliding in and out of your tight little hole?"

"No, Louise, honor bright! It makes me sick to even think of their long ugly snaky things."

"Do you mean to say that you've never used a candle on yourself?"

"Yes, supposing I have? A candle's different. There are no germs shooting into you to put you in a family way and get you all diseased up. I know all about it," she said.

That was no doubt the crux of the whole situation, as most any girl who has never dared savor a prick will admit.

"Well, we'll have more to say about that later, Sylvia," I put in. "How about finishing up what you've started?"

She went down on me once more, in a more businesslike manner this time, separating and then sucking and tonguing the soaking lips. I derived a keen salacious pleasure from the thought that she was unknowingly filling her mouth with that much-feared semen which she wouldn't ordinarly touch with a ten-foot pole, much less allow to be introduced into her cunt on a ten-inch prick. Even when my touchy clitty had been fully aroused by her perverted tonguing and I felt my climax coming on, I held back the gathering flood of pleasure as long as I possibly could—just to keep her working longer. When I finally came, my contracting muscles wrung into her mouth the remains of the emission which she had not already swallowed in her diligent sucking.

"Now it's my turn, Louise," she said, wiping her brimming mouth with the back of her hand, and settling herself comfortably on her back with her white thighs thrown wide apart with expectant abandon. Her cunt, with its fresh pouting vulva, certainly looked good enough even for me to eat; but I had something more substantial in store for her.

"Wait a minute, Sylvia," I said, hopping from the bed, "I have a surprise for you. You know what a dildo is, don't you—one of those rubber things shaped just like a man's? Well, I'm going to try it on you."

"It won't hurt, will it?"

"No; but to make sure, slip this piece of cocoa butter into your cunny. It will soften and lubricate you." I handed her a medicated vaginal suppository and she slipped it up between the scarlet inner lips of her cunt.

Hastening to the bathroom, I released my two ravening lions. Thanks to the warming influence of the picture album I had left with them, not to mention the condition I had left poor Benito in, they were so far gone that theyewere about to bugger each other. I separated them by sheer force and led them into the bedroom. Sylvia, glancing up from her loving occupation, uttered a horrified scream and dived under the covers to hide her nakedness as well as to escape the sight of the two menacing pricks that could not have failed to meet her gaze.

I approached the bed and tore the covers from off her. She lay there cowering and sobbing.

"Listen, Sylvia," I said determinedly, "another such scream and I'll either gag you or chloroform you. Not that anyone outside this apartment could hear you, but my nerves can't stand such screeching. You think that you can sneer superciliously at me, and perhaps carry tales home about my relations with men? Well, you'll have to tell them a few things about yourself, too. Because, whether you like it or not, you're going to get fucked—and right now. And if you don't know what getting fucked means, you're going to learn in just a minute. Benito! Luigi! Come here! Which of you is the hardest? Let me feel . . ."

Again Luigi was the chosen one. I gave him his instructions. Benito and I would each hold her thighs apart while he performed the operation with relentless rapidity. "Remember," I said, "in deflowering a woman, gentleness is no mercy."

"Louise!" screamed Sylvia, choking with horror, "you can't actually mean to have them do that to me? Why it's a crime! It's rape! I'll . . . I'll . . ."

Luigi, during this speech, had brought his affair to her central mark, thanks to the advantageous position in which Benito and I held her for him. A single furious thrust and his staunch scalpel had severed so much of her maidenhead as was left from her lifetime's fingerings and candle-masturbations. Another plunge, and the rest of his throbbing cock sank from sight. As he withdrew for another stab, I was frightened by the sight of the blood upon his weapon. What if he should do her some harm? I would have to answer for it . . . but Sylvia's threatening voice reassured me.

"Louise Smith!" she cried, "I'll have you arrested for this! Oh! Oh! Please take him away! He is killing me! Oh, you beastly man! Get off of me! You are tearing me apart with that dreadful thing of yours. Oh! My whole stomach is split open!"

"Take it and don't complain, Sylvia," I said, unconsciously forming a rhyme, "for if you want the pleasure, you must have the pain."

But she kept right on yelling.

"Will you keep quiet!" I exclaimed impatiently, as I became more and more aroused

224

at the fine sight of Luigi's superb tool, hard and polished as Carrara marble, its veins swelling with an abundance of hot blood, plunging in and out of the juicy folds of her cunt, right before my eyes . . . and I began to decide that I would have done better to keep that fine morsel for myself. "This is the best thing that could ever have happened to you. Here—" I released her thigh and signaled Benito to do likewise — "wrap your legs about the man's back and put a little action into that leaden backside of yours. And one more word out of you and I'll put Benito's prick in your mouth to shut you up!"

She stopped crying, but continued moaning softly—regarding me with infinite hatred in her eyes . . . the ungrateful wretch.

"Come, Benito!" I said, throwing myself accommodatingly on my back beside the raped Sylvia. "You now get yours at last—and *we'll* show them how to do it. I'm sorry I have no more maidenheads to offer, but we'll manage all right without."

The eager young Italian mounted between the firm white flesh of my thighs; but only a moment after he had penetrated into the soft quivering channel of my body, he went off in a premature spasmodic frenzy, deluging my excited crack with his warm creamy spend. However, without pausing, he set off on a second and more prolonged course, during which I came twice. From the corner of my eye I had seen Sylvia watching us with an interest that was increasing as her pain decreased. From disgust her expression soon changed to understanding—as Luigi's various frictionings stirred in her the first echoings of a delight she had never tasted before.

Just as she was apparently beginning to enjoy it, though, Luigi, unable to withstand the overpowering sensations fostered by her tight gripping cunt, reached his climax. As his hot, prolific sperm deluged her wounded quim and the realization of the danger she was being subjected to dawned upon her, Sylvia gave a scream of horror and renewed all her tearful complaints. But Luigi kept right on raping her, this time moving more easily in her well-lubricated sheath, and as Benito was spilling his second load into me at this moment, I let him finish, pushed him from me, and mounting over Sylvia's tearful face, smothered her cowardly wailings with my dripping cunt. She sobbed with hatred and disgust as she choked on the plentiful spendings that dripped down her throat; but as the continued administration of Luigi's peerless prick began to take effect upon her, her lower body began writhing pleasurably, and she was so carried away with lecherous feelings as to begin sucking zestfully upon my spew-bathed joy-pouch. Thus does generosity come to even the meanest creatures during the approach of the supreme enjoyment in fornication—that great humanizer.

When I had given down my own rapturous effusion, I climbed from off her to better watch the superb sight of the finish. Our blushing, protesting maiden had twisted her legs tightly about her assaulter's loins, her arms clinging convulsively to his neck. Her bottom was heaving up to meet his thrusts with passionate abondon, her whole body vibrating in a frenzy of mad desire.

*"S'arrete, Luigi!"* I cried at this point. "Stop a moment!"

Luigi obeyed with extreme reluctance.

"Now, Miss Watson," I addressed the quivering bit of humanity nailed to my bed by Luigi's stiff cock, "I am beginning to regret my taking advantage of you. I shall have your torturer desist at once."

But such a reproachful and appealing glance came from her feverish joy-clouded eyes, that cruel as I felt, I could not bring myself to deprive her of that rod, that staff, which comforted her.

"Go ahead, Luigi," I directed resignedly, "give it to her." And as Benito was by now presenting himself with an entirely resurrected hard-on, I stretched myself face down on the wide bed, and to shock my initiate rather than anything else, let him force his way into my narrow rear crevice and revel in my tightly fitting fundament.

The best of things must end, and before long we all had had—not enough, but all that we could stand. I dismissed the two men immediately, and leading Sylvia to the bathroom, loaned her my douching syringe to make her vaginal toilette.

When she came out, I offered her my hand cordially.

"No ill feelings I hope, Sylvia," I said. "It's really all for the best."

She turned her back sullenly—and quickly putting on her ugly clothes once more, the ungrateful wretch left me without a word.

The very next day however, she paid me an unexpected visit at my hotel rooms.

"Those men aren't around, are they?" she asked, peering into my bedroom.

"No," I reassured her.

She was visibly disappointed. She had come to get the name and address of the man who had violated her, she told me rather curtly.

"And what do you want that for, my dear Sylvia?" I asked.

"Oh, don't be a fool, Louise!" she snapped. "If I should be in a family way, I suppose I have the right to know the name of the father of my child, haven't I?"

I laughed and told her of the contraceptive suppository that she had unknowingly used. "If you want to try it again, though, here's Benito's business card. I suppose he can lead you to Luigi—or take pretty good care of you himself."

She took the card and stalked out haughtily, without so much as thanking me.

Some months later it came to my ears that when she returned to the United States, the great well-equipped Italian went with her—undoubtedly, at her own expense. Such can be the irresistible allure of a strong cock even to one who, before its proper introduction to her, couldn't even think of one without turning sick.

# CHAPTER THIRTEEN

After a few more days in Rome I started north, stopping over at Florence for a while—where, to put it hastily, I was deliciously back-scuttled by moonlight on the Ponte Vecchio, that same bridge over the Arno where old Dante met his Beatrice—and, if history may be disregarded a bit, probably did the same for her as was done for me.

From here I proceeded to Venice, the lovely watery stamping grounds of that full-testicled Casanova whose female reincarnation I sometimes like to think myself. Did I try fucking in a gondola? the eager reader asks. I didn't miss—and let me say, there's nothing like it. The gentle graceful motion of the boat seems to be intended just for the rhythms of coition, the gondoliers are the very embodiment of discretion, and if one can't get in enough fucking by night, there are always deserted canals and fully enclosed gondolas that permit action at any time of day. To lie in love's delicious lethargy while floating on some lazy lagoon, to the accompaniment of the gondolier's sensuous intoning of some Neapolitan tune—ah, this is paradise!

Then further north into Germany, with a stop at Munich for a few days. And here let me disappoint the friendly reader as I was disappointed. Munich is the only city on the Continent which I have visited without getting pushed. There the bellies of the populace are so distended with beer-drinking that fucking is, if not impossible, at least a most discouraging thing to contemplate.

Then to Berlin—a visit that I had been postponing for some time. One of my first acts was to look up my old friend Bob, who, you will remember, had been dragged away to Germany just about the time when he might have had my maiden flower. He was pretty much the same now as then—only more romantic and impractical than ever. If anything, I was the only one of us who had matured.

He was not living with his wealthy parents any longer, he told me, preferring to enact the part of the impecunious bohemian, suffering for his "art," knocking around, painting a little, writing bad poetry on occasion and playing the violin to soothe his anguished soul. We did not hit it up so well together—although he still professed to be madly in love with me. Sentimentality was what I had outgrown and he had yielded to completely.

One gorgeous June evening we went together to the Tiergarten, Berlin's beautiful public park. We drank beer and listened to music for a while. In the intervals he read to me some Baudelaire from a volume which he always carried with him now in place of the Keats of former days. I know my Baudelaire perfectly in French and in English: in the German it sounded nothing less than barbarous.

After a while, we wandred off into the dark wooded groves where the atmosphere was heavy with the redolent perfumes of roses and honeysuckles. He made love to me. To his naive poetic soul, I was still a virgin. He regretted those past days, he told me, when he had taken unfair advantage of my inexperience; yet it became clear that with his increasing amorousness he would sue for a renewal of those privileges. I liked him and of course it would have been the easiest thing in the world for me to give him all that he craved and then some. But there was a beautiful hopelessness in his voice, a poetic aura in which he enwrapped me, that made me feel it would be sacrilegious to allow it to be resolved down to "mere" fornication.

Standing under the trees, I allowed him to put his arms about me and kiss me. But when he dropped to his knees before me and began caressing my thighs and buttocks, I shook him off and ran back a few steps to avoid him, feeling foolish enough in this unaccustomed prudery of mine and yet feeling that it was the thing expected of me.

He followed me on his knees until the brambles of a bush catching in my dress arrested my further retreat.

He disentangled me, and still on his knees, passed his feverish hands up under my perfumed skirts. I wore no underthings and stood in a momentary quandary. Pushing up my dress, he buried his hot face high on my bare thighs, holding me to him with his hands on my naked posteriors.

I could feel his panting breath on the damp gates of my cunny. My mind went back for a moment to that day in the woods when I had first met him, when he had buried his head in my lap just so . . . . A feeling of tenderness pervaded me. I rested my hand upon his curly hair. I experienced that same excitement of having him so close to my cunny—and yet knowing that to tongue it would doubtless be the last thing on earth that would enter his mind.

But to my surprise—and yes, horror—for I

was still transported back to those virginal days—he pressed his mouth to the very quick, and inserting his tongue between the full luscious lips, began lapping me—unmistakably. I tried to push him away, but he held on desperately. Soon I found my thighs unconsciously relaxing and easing apart to allow his velvety tongue to get into me further.

"So!" I thought to myself resignedly, "the rogue knows what he's doing after all. He'll excite me so much with his tongue that I just won't be able to refuse him when he offers to finish up with his prick." But if that had been his original intention, he overstepped it, for even when the success of his maneuver became apparent by my wildly quivering body and low voluptuous cries, he kept right on lapping me—till the climax came and passed. Weak and trembling, I let him draw me down beside him on the grass.

"Did you like it?" he panted—a bit foolishly, I thought.

"Yes—of course—it was nice."

"Then, my darling, my goddess, let me love you! Yield your divine body to me entirely!" Speaking tremendously, he brought out his stiff part, no considerable affair in the light of the many others I had encountered since last I had seen it. There still seemed to be a note of uncertainty in his voice. It did not flatter me —at least not in my physical being—and I wasn't going to make up his mind for him. And the thought of all his poetic ideals, his exaggerated estimate of my chastity and my worth—all made me ashamed to yield to him —unwilling to destroy his illusions with the carnal earthiness of a fuck. Surely, I reasoned,

232

after all his dreams, my cunt, nice as it might be, could only be a disappointment. And anyway, I was quite sated, what with his injudicious gamahuching and with the nice tussle I had had that same afternoon with a hotel bellboy who had come up to deliver a telegram and found me in my bath.

I drew my skirts down and pushed him gently from me.

"Please!" he pleaded, approaching me once more and nestling his excited part in my hand.

"No, Bob," I expostulated softly, unconsciously stroking the velvety warm cylinder of flesh, "I couldn't possibly give myself to you. Yes—as you said before—we were young and foolish when we played with each other years ago the way we did. I am trying to forget that now, and you must help me. No—the man I give myself to will be the man I choose over all other men—the man I marry." And silently I continued stroking his stiff smooth instrument, as if lost in reverie.

The expected climax was not long in coming. Suddenly he threw his arms about my neck, sobbing, "Oh, you pure, unattainable woman!"

I drew my skirt discreetly out of danger, and turned his spouting weapon downward to the grass—feeling only then a slight qualm of regret at the waste of the dear warm fluid that I can never get enough of. With faked ingenuousness I pretended that what had happened was entirely accidental—nevertheless, he was profoundly grateful.

As he ushered me back to my hotel later that evening, we noticed a considerable crowd gathered in front of the French embassy making some hostile demonstration. The relations between Germany and France, according to the newspapers, had been becoming more and more strained. I decided to curtail my stay in Berlin and return to my beloved Paris the very next day.

Paris from that summer onward, with somber war clouds hovering over all Europe, was a place of rather forced and unnatural gaiety. The shadow of possible death hung over the head of almost every man that sought our arms. But we did "our bit"—in our own way—exerting all our powers to make our friends and patrons forget the morrow, and yet when that morrow came to have them look back on our day with the satisfaction of having lived life to its fullest.

The pressing demand upon us became greater and greater. There was no one now whom we could turn away from our doors in clear conscience. More and more recruits became necessary to fill our lists, more space, more houses. Before long I found myself, entirely against my will, all too well known a wholesale trafficker in female flesh. When the government sent out a call for an organized group of women for the complaisance of the men at the front, my friends in the official bureaus veritably forced the contact upon me, and I was compelled to nearly kill myself rounding up scores of healthy women to send to the towns behind the lines to keep our boys happy and fit. Without half needing it or desiring it, I was becoming wealthy hand over fist—with money pouring in from more branch houses, public or private enterprises, than Fleurette and I could keep track of.

Borne aloft on a wave of patriotism, I was,

for a time earlier in the war, actually induced to undertake a commission for the secret Intelligence Division which took me into Belgium and the enemy territory. Only the recentness of the great conflict prevents me from divulging the exact nature of my errand. But suffice it to say, to dispel any budding romantic notion on the part of the reader, that as a spy I was a total failure. Falling into the hands of a company of German soldiers while masquerading as a simple Belgium maid, I was raped, or rather gang-fucked—for I put up no very strenuous resistance—by 18 privates in succession. Had not two officers returned from a prolonged absence to disperse the men and make the 19th and 20th, Lord knows what might have happened to me. As it was, when they finished, my cunt was almost in a pulp. For the reader may take my word for it, that while the first four or five were very nice and the next two or three were bearable, the rest were decidedly unpleasant. For once in my life I had more than enough.

Having learned only that Teutonic pricks are on the whole bigger and thicker than Gallic ones, and this being a discovery of no particular value to my country in winning the war, I resigned my commission and returned to Paris, where I could do much more good, I thought, being fucked by our allies rather than by our enemies.

But let me hasten on to the end of the war, and with the approach of the date of my present writing, the end of my story.

With the armistice, Paris became once more the joyous center of the world of pleasure, with people pouring in from every country of the globe to celebrate the awakening from the four-year nightmare that had been ours. Wine flowed and joy reigned supreme once more. Gladly I closed down or sold out my subsidiary houses and concentrated all my lavishness and attention on the one that I occupy now, making it the most exclusive and desirable house of rendezvous in this most desirable city of the world.

With the Peace Conference, which was only about six months ago, when I first began penning these fond foolish lines, the greatest men of every nation gathered here in Paris. There was scarcely one that I did not have the honor of entertaining intimately during that period here in my luxurious establishment. When I first began these memoirs I must confess it was in the boastful mood of telling of my relations with all these celebrities. But my tale even in its simpler aspects has been—I hope —so interesting, and—yes, I fear—so lengthy, that I have decided to awake no regrets in the hearts of generous thighs, to cause no embarrassment to any who have shared my hospitality—no, not to them, nor to their friends, descendants or copatriots—for I realize that the world that exists outside the walls of my bounteous mansion on the Boulevard Haussmann is not the same unashamed world as exists within.

# CHAPTER FOURTEEN

Dear reader, the parting of our ways draws nigh. But before you leave these pages, before you leave *me*, perhaps never to return, I would have you spend just one more joyous evening with me at the Maison Madeleine. Any evening—a typical evening—just yesterday evening will do.

I come from my (private) boudoir where I have just enjoyed a long refreshing nap and a cool bath to prime me for the evening's pleasant exertions. I am already thirty, the reader will remember, and a bit plump from my luxurious living; but my years sit lightly on my shoulders—my admirers swear that I look no more than twenty-six at most.

I greet my many friends who are already assembled and have a kiss for each of my faithful girls, every one of whom is bright and smiling and at her very best tonight. They are wearing—not slovenly kimonos, as one might expect—but the very finest evening gowns that the studios of Poiret can afford.

Monsier "Quatrefois," an elderly but wealthy patron of ours, so-named by us because while he has the greatest difficulty raising a hard-on for even a single round of love's battle, he is continually entertaining us with accounts of how in his younger days he never hit less than four times running—calls me aside to tell me a new smutty story that he has already retailed to all present. Also he brings me good news of an investment in some South American bonds he has made for me.

A light luncheon with many sparkling wines

and stimulating liqueurs is being served by
two of my most attractive maids, both of
them dressed in maddeningly prim dresses
that make them appear, though desirable, as
severe as cloistered nuns—and as unattainable. One of them is tonight to be admitted
to our ranks as a fully commissioned dispen-
ser of pleasure—but this feature of the evening is reserved for later.

My good wine soon banishes that slight
restraint that can exist at the very outset
even in such a place as ours. The conversation becomes more lively; but without taking
too loose or vulgar a turn. The genuine sy-
barite knows better than to evaporate the
imagination of words in advance of action and
thus secularize the sacred mysteries of love.
Here and there, of course, a breast or thigh
is uncovered to be kissed or fondled; but the
radical instruments of amorous warfare are by
both sexes kept discreetly out of sight until
the actual tender hostilities should begin. By
thus concealing the exact extent of their arm-
ament, an element of conjecture and suspense
is added to the number of other pleasant
emotions that charge the perfumed atmosphere.

Our spacious drawing room, I might say for
the benefit of those readers who have never
visited my maison, is brightly illuminated by
concealed nonglaring electric lights. The furniture is luxuriously adapted to meet the
demand of the most precise and specialized
voluptuary. On the floor is spread an extra-
ordinarily thick and expensive Persian rug
that in itself makes a couching place as soft
and comfortable as anyone could wish—and

in addition there are innumerable cushions and hassocks of varying sizes and consistencies strewn about, making possible any arrangement, any elevation that might be desired. In the center of the floor there is a huge cushioned dais, all of fifteen feet long and ten feet wide, and so much of the available wall space as is not occupied by my well-stocked buffet is lined with large sofas and ingenious reclining chairs. Doors lead off to the dining room, two dressing rooms with baths, and three retiring rooms. In the luxurious reception hall, where we sometimes hold dances or special functions, there are *ascenseurs* leading to the upper stories, our numerous private chambers and our living quarters.

Someone remarks that it is time the concert should begin, for, he adds laughingly, he fancies all the instruments are in tune. I give the signal to begin, for I have a most delightful novelty to present to my guests tonight. Yesterday we played a new game called "Put and Take" – employing a large dice-top, marked "Put one," "Take one," "Put Two," "Take Two," "Take All," and so on. Everybody would spin in turn, alternating according to sex. For each "put," a male player would be allowed just one intimate stroke within the cunny of his partner. A "take" gave him the privilege of planting just one sucking kiss at the same place. A female player would win corresponding privileges over her male partner. A "take all" authorized the player to do just that, retiring from the game with any partner of his or her choice and collecting his winnings within sight of everyone;—but as a "take all" occurred only at long intervals in the game, the reader can imagine to what a pitch of excitement the players were worked up, forced to content themselves with one or two sucks at a time. Ultimately, of course, every player made a "take all"; but picture the feverish plight of the last few players after almost two hours of gambling. One couple made enough "puts" and "takes" to reach a complete orgasm by installments—and when the last two survivors spun again and again without making the desired "take all," we who had long since expended our winnings, were favored with the ludicrous sight of the interlocked couple spinning the top, taking a shove or two, spinning once more, and so on to the end. The game was an uproarious success.

But for tonight, as I have said, I have invented something different. I call it "Cunt Polo." A wide spotless sheet is spread over the center dais, and Manon and Rosa, undressing quickly, lie nude on their backs with their legs wide apart and the soles of their feet pressed together—thus forming a fascinating diamond of plump shapely limbs. Now I called for four male volunteers. A number of American college boys, wealthy and devilish, who are with us tonight, come forward immediately. I ask them to strip. which they do unhesitantly, bringing to light fine weapons that are just raring for adventure of any sort.

Two of them, under my direction, take their places in reverse, or "69," positions over my two pretty assistants, respectively lodging their members in the mouths of the girls, who however make no active move until I give the signal for the game to start. The pretty cunts that crown each apex of this charming double triangle are the goals. The vigorous young men lying with their mouths conveniently near are to be the guards. The other two men are to be the opposing field players, and a large brandied maraschino cherry is to be the ball or chukker.

The players choose their sides for the first quarter as I explain the rules to them. With tongues as the only implements of play, each is to attempt to get the ball between the glistening posts of his opponent's goal. The guards are of course to protect their goals with their tongues. But what complicates the game is the fact that the two girls are meanwhile to suck upon the instruments of their riders, and the quarter is to end whenever any one of the players should go off, whether voluntarily or involuntarily.

The game starts amid the encouraging shouts of the numerous spectators. Mock bets are being placed. But I shall not describe the game in too great detail. Suffice it that there is much bumping of heads on the part of the two men fighting for the ball in the field and much frenzied cunt-tonguing on the part of the respective guards whenever the ball shows any signs of approaching the fleshy goals. The first quarter ends most unexpectedly with one of the "goals" going off—that is, my passionate Manon—and a heated discussion ensues as to whether this is to end the quarter or not. I rule that the game cannot continue so long as anyone is in the throes of pleasure.

The goals are changed and the game proceeds. Within the very first few minutes of play, one of the guards becomes so distracted with the naughty little love-bites with which Rosa favors his organ that he allows two goals to be made against him; but just at this moment Manon does as much for her superincumbent. His panting mouth is unable to protect his goal, the score is evened and the quarter ends as Manon proudly pulls a spouting cock from her mouth.

Now we observe a short intermission in which refreshing drinks are passed around. Before proceeding with the second half we find it necessary to put two new guards in the game. All the girls want to be goalposts, but I decide to keep the same ones in. The play resumes, but suddenly comes to a standstill in the third quarter. Where is the ball? As referee I intervene and search between the lips of the two darling goals. No sign of it. Then one of the field-men confesses shamefacedly that in the excitement of the game he swallowed it! I fetch another cherry and put it into play. But something is the matter with this same blundering player. He muffs the ball and allows his rival the entire field. Were it not for some remarkable play on the part of his goalkeeper, his team would be heavily scored against. But the reason comes out and the quarter comes to an end when we find the pathetic young man has come off in his trousers—what with the unaccustomed proximity of all this luscious cunt.

The last quarter starts off with some rapid field play. The score being tied so far, everyone is anxious to see the final result. The ball is now heading for Manon's goal . . . that was almost a touchdown!—but her guard repulses the bit of fruit nobly. It caroms against her white thigh and goes shooting across the field toward Rosa's cunt. The two field men rush to the spot and dribble the ball back and forth against her satiny flesh, dangerously close to the goal, battling for the possession of it. Closer and closer to the gaping scarlet goalpost it comes, every inch of territory desperately contested. It all depends on the goalkeeper now! But he is panting with the excitement not only of the game but of the lovely concentrated assault that he is receiving at the lips of Rosa at his other end—and though he is moving his tongue bravely back and forth, he is doing it blindly . . . he is too far afield, high up over the clitty, and not over the lower part of the goal. The breathless spectators lean over, watching anxiously. The cherry is maneuvered to the very lips of the cunt. It is a certain touchdown . . . but no— just as the powerful tongue of the opponent presses the cherry for a straightaway to the goal over the infinitesmal remaining distance, Rosa suddenly doubles up in the delicious agony of spending, throws up her legs and wraps them about her lover's neck. The field of battle is wiped out, and the player headed with the ball for her cunny, meets up only with her tiny wrinkled anus. The game is over in a riot of hearty laughter as both Rosa and her cunt's guardian finish off the superb 69 in each other's mouths.

While we stand about refreshing ourselves with cocktails and more liqueurs, Janet and some handsome young man who is a frequent applicant for her favors regale us with a gracious and voluptuous exhibition waltz. One of the girls plays the piano, and as they dance slowly about the room her partner undoes her dress, disclosing to our view a pair of finely molded delicious twin-orbs. Then, without interrupting the dance, he removes her gown altogether. Her step-ins are loosened and kicked off without one false move and now the whole company is dazzled and delighted at the sight of her exquisitely fashioned thighs and buttocks, which, disclosed to us so rhythmically, and with the accompaniment of the sensuous music, can not help but be doubly effective. As the number draws to a close, her gallant whips out a master member whose eminent size and goodly shape at once proclaims the owner a true hero among women, and as with the final chords of the selection the accomplished Janet springs up into his arms and wraps her lithe legs about his waist, he catches her ready cunt upon the upstanding head of his part and carries her gracefully to a nearby couch where he falls upon her and concludes and augments the pleasure of the dance with a vigorous to-and-fro motion that soon brings on the ultimate melting dissolution for both of them.

But there is yet the important business of the evening to attend to. I introduce our newest enlistment, Mimi, to the assembled company and offer her choice between a public and a private initiation.

"In wishing to enter your service, madame," she replies modestly, "I wish to please the greatest number of people in the greatest possible way. My only fear is that my comparative inexperience will make me appear at a disadvantage among all these beautiful girls."

"Well spoken, my darling," I say, kissing

her reassuringly. "Your inexperience is what will delight us most."

The lucky man who has been chosen in advance as her liberator steps forward and, with extreme relish, deprives her piece by piece of her convent-like habiliments which heretofore she has worn as a contrast for the more desirable impudicity of us whom soon she is to join. To the charms of her flashing eyes, pouting mouth and little retrouse nose are now added those of her bare shoulders, the curves floating away into her shapely arms and soft tapering fingers—fingers made especially for the delicious manipulation of the sensitive phalluses of hot-blooded men. Then with the removal of her chemise comes into view two dazzling white opulent globes of firm flesh, each topped with a dainty rose, and a soft polished belly, sweeping down in a majestic curve like a broad paradisical plateau and relieved in its center by a maddeningly coquettish little dimple of a navel. Then the majestic columns of her matchless thighs, adorned at their sweet intersection with the delicious rosy cleft of flesh, the spring of love, bowered in dark silky foliage.

In accordance with a rather strange procedure of initiation, insisted upon by some of the more imaginative and sentimental clients, I, as the mother superior of this temple dedicated to the worship of pleasure, must hold the initiate upon my lap during the whole inaugural ceremony. Changing into a light negligee, I take my place upon the couch in a semireclining position with a number of silk cushions beneath me. Mimi lies on her back upon my soft generous body, and as I have taken care to open my peignoir all the way up the front, I can feel her bare satiny skin upon my naked lap and bosom.

We both spread wide our thighs, hers somewhat slim but perfect, mine decidedly more voluptuous and ample. The celebrant approaches, wearing a dressing robe which he hurriedly removes, displaying to us the proud proof of his manhood, stiff and upstanding, threatening the very skies with its pleasing power, its kingly acorn-shaped (but by no means acorn-sized!) head, broad and shelving, purple and distended with the blood pressure of his vigorous state. As he comes between our outstretched thighs, he compliments me prettily by confessing that between the two fine cunts before him he is in a quandary which to choose.

"Who told you you were to choose at all, young man!" I chide him with mock severity. "Attend to your business!" And from my position of supreme vantage, I pass my hands down over that smoothest, whitest, roundest belly to that soft groove which kind nature has stamped there between two crimson, fleshy ridges for the mutual delectation of man and woman. Gently spreading the lips of that luscious nether mouth with one hand, I with my other lay hold of the staunch velvety officiator and approach that dear idol so worshiped by women to its true and proper niche. Forcefully he shoves it in. While Mimi, according to the rules of the house, comes to us without her maidenhead, it is obvious that she has disposed of it with her finger or a candle, and that this is her very first penetration by man. With all the delicious difficulty of a defloration, we see his tumescent part sink into the tight scarlet crack inch by inch until it is entirely out of sight, sunk in the tight moist folds of her lush laboratory of love. The poor dear winces at first, but with the hypnotizing effect of her master's slow to-and-fro movement, she is soon roused to active participation. Then, under the stinging lash of pleasure, she is unable to contain herself. Throwing her arms and legs about wildly, she heaves to meet his eager thrusts, twists and writhes upon her stiff, fleshy axis—at that moment indeed the very center of her world. The breathing of both is now swift and laborious, the tumult of their senses as evidenced by the tumult of their bodies keeps rising to higher and higher pitch. To save myself from his, to me, useless pounding, and to give them more freedom of movement, I slip out from under Mimi's quivering form. A moment later, with sudden stiffening, she stretches out, a soft shudder runs through her pleasure-convulsed frame, and they both lay motionless, dying with that dear delight, an occasional spasmodic movement or a soulful melting sigh being the only signs of life they show.

By this time, needless to say, all my friends and clients—and not excluding myself—are sufficiently wound up by the spectacles of the evening to themselves wish to participate. Some of them, indeed, accustomed to the privileges of my house, have not waited for the last act, but have taken possession of sofas—and girls— to themselves stage their own little tableaux and dramas. But there are other more dignified and self-conscious patrons present, who, while enjoying the sight of the others' enjoyments would not think of taking their own pleasure in public. And so, though my strongest urge is to grab a man and hurry off into some corner, I must pair them off with my girls for private tête-à-têtes—like the captain of a burning ship at sea, saving myself for the last. And then, when I finally get to the end of my roster of guests, I find that there are two men remaining, with room for only one in my lifeboat . . .

"Baron F., you will come with me. Now, Monsieur C., I am sorry, but if you will wait just a few minutes, Henriette will soon be down to take care of you."

"But Madame! It is with you that I wish to be. Perhaps the baron, if he has no special preference, will be willing to cede priority to me."

*"Mais non, monsieur!"* the baron bristles, "I am leaving Paris in a few hours, and this is my last opportunity, my farewell, with Madame!"

"But Madame!" Monsieur C. expostulates, "did you not give me your solemn promise last week that the very next time . . . "

"Gentlemen, gentlemen! Please, gentlemen!" I exclaimed distraughtly. "What can I do? Must you resort to something like dueling or cutting a pack of cards to determine which of you is to have me?"

*"Sacre nom!"* the baron puts in, "I'll tell you what. We are both gentlemen. We shall be friends. If Madame Madeleine has no objections, and if you are willing, monsieur, we shall all retire together—*a trois, comprenez-vous?"*

"Oh, gentlemen!" I cry, overwhelmed, but nevertheless pleased by this friendly solution.

We repair to one of the most luxurious of

my private chambers. When I turn around after switching on the lights, I am confronted with two stiff peters, leveled at me by my two guests respectively.

"Hands up!" the baron exclaims in laughable English.

"Your cunny or your life!" shouts Monsieur C., catching the spirit—and they make for me —both on burglary bent. (Yes, I said burglary.)

"Now, gentlemen, no squabbling," I urge as we tumble upon the spacious bed and they rifle my secret treasures and charms. "Let us all undress and then we'll divide the swag evenly." They comply, and I too divest myself hurriedly both of my clothes and my dignity. By now I am hot enough to want to be raped by the Eiffel Tower.

"You, Baron," I say to this personage as he turns to me stripped of everything but his monocle, "lie back here near the edge of the bed." He does so. I climb over him, and bringing the head of his stiff tool to the dewy lips of my furry, satin-lined muff, I let it sink into me to the utmost extent of its delicious powers of penetration.

Monsieur C. stands by with disappointment written on all his features, wondering no doubt where his share is to come from. I set his mind at rest immediately, however, and find "penal" servitude for the naked symbol of his manhood by having him oil it first with some scented pomade, and then, as I lie forward over the baron, allowing him to step up behind and slip it in between the jutting cheeks of my posterior and into my tight but willing *cul*.

As his erect staff slides into that part of me,

made additionally narrow by the close proximity of the other bulky distender just to the other side of the thin membrane that separates the cunt from the rectum, I can feel their two members rub against each other in friendly fashion through the negligible intervening partition. Exulting not only in the delicious well-stuffed sensation, but also in the unusual lasciviousness of my doubly spitted position, gorged with a double share of the "dearest morsel of the earth," I feel like some high goddess, uniting in the mystic bond of my body, two men, a nobleman and a commoner, who but for me would not know each other.

However, it is not the metaphysical overtones of my salacious, truly two-horned "dilemma" that long engrosses me. My itching clitty clamors for its tribute. And so, our bodies linked together in this position, all the more delightful because of its difficulty, stretched almost to breaking on this double rack of joy, I start giving them the proper motion. How can I convey to you, dear reader, the incomparable feeling as that local frenzy spread through all my body, putting me almost entirely out of my mind with a furious lust that my two partners might perhaps equal, but certainly not surpass. As back and forth I fuck, as the one of them rams fiercely into my rear while I rise up on the stiff sensitive staff of the other only to come down on it again, both of the favorite parts of my ravenous body are in turn engorged or partially evacuated in an indescribable feverish alternation of attacks and caresses.

Now they crush me mercilessly between them, timing their lunging strokes together instead of in succession, their active loins quivering with the violence of their super-heavenly conflict (for indeed heaven could hold no bliss like this!). I feel the waves of pleasure surging, foaming, raging to a height, inundating all my senses, all my faculties. That critical delirium of supreme felicity that all the pages of my volume have not, I fear, even begun to do justice to, is almost at hand. In wild transports I throw myself about, sob, moan, protest against the extreme pleasure. My stiff-mettled partners drive all the more tempestuously, batter me more cruelly in the blind lust of their own approaching orgasms. Yet it is not mercy that I desire—oh, no! I sob and cry because I would want this divine ecstasy of the senses to last forever—yes, forever, this tremendous cataclysmic pleasure which, if at its height, it lasted five minutes instead of five seconds, would kill even the sturdiest of humans!

Lifted then by the mounting waves of delirious sensation to the highest pitch of joy that life can bear, I am poised for a moment at the sweet terrific critical point—and then suddenly, all the sluices of my body are opened up, all my being, all my soul is dissolved in bliss and poured down into that sensitive passage where escape luckily is denied it by reason of that part being so effectively and deliciously plugged up. And almost simultaneously, with savage cries of triumph, my two riders cram into me the utmost fraction of their flesh that I can engulf and with ungovernable impetuosity hurl into me their joint loads of scalding love fluid. I feel the hot pearly elixir spurt from both sides, flooding both my orifices, spreading into my joy-knotted bowels, mingling with my own pleasurable effusions. Some few more moments of tremulous, convulsive shuddering, the delicious conjunction of our bodies is ended, and we collapse upon the bed, spent, drenched with pleasure, gasping for breath, completely vanquished by love's bounty, and yet resting only so that we may recover strength to resume the stirring of those exquisite vibrations of sensation that tremble still on the strings of delight . . .

# CHAPTER FIFTEEN

That was yesterday, dear reader, and tonight is another night. But though we can go on loving so long as there is life and health in us and still find ever renewed delights in the exercise of that divine function, we cannot go on writing about it indefinitely.

I have, I believe, kept my promise to tell about myself, even more thoroughly than I had originally intended. Perhaps I have even succeeded in somehow justifying myself—although, I hasten to add, it has been my purpose throughout to vindicate not myself but the human body, enchained through centuries by hypocrisy and false modesty.

It was just half a year ago that I began confiding my life to these sympathetic incensorious pages. It was then early spring. It is now late summer. I am seated in the spacious garden behind my house, basking in the sunlight which in Paris is of a brighter gold than anywhere else in the world—and feeling once more that exuberance which begot this arduous scriptorial enterprise of mine. I glance along the high walls that surround my garden, the arbors and nooks that have witnessed so many delightful fetes during the past summer. I drink in my surroundings with a happy sense of possession. I have brought my record at last down to this very living moment. I need only one final thought with which to close these pages, a send-off for the kind and tolerant reader who has lived through so much with me, who has endured the many deficiencies of my unpracticed writing.

·From within the house I hear the happy chatter of my girls, and the blithesome voice of Fleurette singing some haunting ballad of her native province as she goes about her work of social secretary. Would it be too much a cliché to say that we are all one big happy family? Well, it must stand—for we are just that.

But as I grope for my farewell words, I see an interruption coming. A little street urchin has climbed to the top of our wall and is regarding me curiously. My writing can wait—life cannot. I will call him, and perhaps he will furnish me with the ending for my book. . .

I am back again, dear reader, all out of breath and still without that closing thought. Life moves on apace. Things happen more rapidly than I can record them. Shall I tell you what happened? I needn't of course; but I will not leave the reader's curiosity unassuaged.

I called the lad down from the wall. He came to me timidly. He was no more than 13 years old and possessed that bright insolence characteristic of his kind. I like little boys and I was in a state of especial good will. I asked him to name to me anything at all that would make him happy.

"To touch your pretty titties, mam'zelle," he replied brazenly, pointing to where my loose peignoir drooped open a bit.

I was vastly amused, and anxious to measure the extent of his precocity.

"*Mechant!* Naughty boy!" I laughed; but I granted his request.

"*Ces-ci sont tres jolis, tres interessantes,*" (These are very pretty, very interesting), he murmured importantly as he fondled my luxurious curves, rather roughly.

"And have you anything interesting to show me?" I asked.

"Certainly," he replied, "I'll show you my great big 'little brother.'"

I agreed, and with a swaggering air he brought out his youthful organ — the merest plaything of a boy.

"Why that—that isn't very interesting," I told him teasingly. "I'd call that rather small."

"Small, hell!" he retorted bellicosely, "just play with it awhile and see how big it gets. I'll bet if you'd let me shove it into you, you'd say it was big!"

"Come then, you young braggart," I put in, "I'll call your bluff." And leading him to a sheltered arbor where we would be unseen, I threw myself in a hammock and opened my negligee. He was frightened at first and confessed that though he had once tried it on his elder sister, he had never really done it before. I took him upon my bosom and bestowed upon him the first and sweetest joys of his coming manhood.

And now I really must bid the reader adieu —ere something else occurs to demand inclusion in this book of life and to stretch it out indefinitely.

Oftentimes I have wondered—have even been rather pleasantly appalled—at the thought of the great number of fucks that have fallen to my happy lot. At such times I have regretted not having kept some tally of the exact number of passengers of every age and estate that have traveled to paradise on my heaving body.

Twelve centuries before Christ cast his dark stigma of impotence upon the world, Cheops, an Egyptian monarch, ordered his beautiful daughter to take to prostitution to replenish his dwindling treasury. She, wishing to leave a monument to herself, besought each of her numerous lovers to present her with a single stone to be employed for that purpose. Her pyramid still stands outside of Cairo—only all the resources of modern science have failed to estimate even the approximate number of stones in that immense pile. So inexhaustible is the marvelous joy-giving power of woman...

As for myself, dear reader, I desire no such immortality. To be remembered pleasantly for a while by all those many who have tasted of joy between my thighs in one way or another is all that I would ask. And as for all you who know me only through the medium of these pages, I can but conclude at last by saying that every hard-on raised during the reading of this book (even if it be doused immediately in soft female flesh or destroyed by hand), will be a monument of the noblest sort erected to my memory.

## THE END

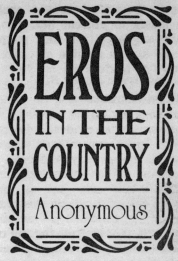

Headline books are available at your bookshop or newsagent, or can be ordered from the following address:

Headline Book Publishing PLC
Cash Sales Department
PO Box 11
Falmouth
Cornwall
TR10 9EN
England

UK customers please send cheque or postal order (no currency), allowing 60p for postage and packing for the first book, plus 25p for the second book and 15p for each additional book ordered up to a maximum charge of £1.90 in UK.

BFPO customers please allow 60p for postage and packing for the first book, plus 25p for the second book and 15p per copy for the next seven books, thereafter 9p per book.

Overseas and Eire customers please allow £1.25 for postage and packing for the first book, plus 75p for the second book and 28p for each subsequent book.